TELL ME NO LIES

An unexpected visit from the police to inform her that her aunt, her only living relative, had been murdered, was not the sort of birthday present Angela Divine wanted. She was relieved, then shocked, when told she did not have to identify the body because it had already been done — by Grace's stepson. But Grace did not have a stepson, so who had come forward with that claim? Ultimately it would be her aunt's little dog that would provide the key to the mystery . . .

Books by Louise Pakeman
Published by The House of Ulverscroft:

THE PUMPKIN SHELL
CHANGE OF SKIES
FLOWERS FOR THE JOURNEY
A PINCH OF SUGAR
LOVE'S HERITAGE

LOUISE PAKEMAN

◆

TELL ME NO LIES

Complete and Unabridged

ULVERSCROFT
Leicester

First published in Great Britain in 2009 by
Robert Hale Limited
London

First Large Print Edition
published 2009
by arrangement with
Robert Hale Limited
London

British Library CIP Data

Pakeman, Louise, 1936 –
 Tell me no lies.
 1. Detective and mystery stories.
 2. Large type books.
 I. Title
 823.9'2–dc22

ISBN 978–1–84782–936–8

Published by
F. A. Thorpe (Publishing)
Anstey, Leicestershire
Set by Words & Graphics Ltd.
Anstey, Leicestershire
Printed and bound in Great Britain by
T. J. International Ltd., Padstow, Cornwall

This book is printed on acid-free paper

1

It was a second or two before I realized that the bell that had dragged me from a deep sleep was not my weekday alarm but someone pressing my doorbell. With their finger glued to it, I thought glumly, as I pushed my feet into my slippers and groped for a robe. It was Sunday morning, for goodness' sake — who on earth? Malcolm perhaps, or a delivery of flowers for my birthday. With that hopeful thought I remembered today was my birthday and feeling more cheerful I hurried to answer the summons.

My happy expectation was replaced with clammy dread as I opened the door. Policewomen, I knew, did not call early in the morning simply to wish one a happy birthday.

'Angela Divine?'

Bereft of speech, I could only nod.

'May I come in?'

I unfroze sufficiently to nod again. With fumbling fingers I unhooked the chain from the door and stepped back into the tiny vestibule of my small ground-floor flat. I gulped and pressed myself against the wall to allow the policewoman to squeeze past me.

I crossed the two steps into the tiny kitchen area separated from the lounge by a breakfast bar. There I stopped, rested one hand on the bar for support and faced her.

'Grace Arbuthnot of The Treasure Chest was your aunt?'

I nodded again. While one part of my mind was registering the past tense, at the same time, with another, I could hear my aunt remarking, with some asperity, '*Cat got your tongue, girl?*' I swallowed and at last managed to croak. 'Yes — yes, she is.'

The policewoman gestured vaguely in the direction of one of the pinewood stools. A lifelong respect for the law prompted me to pull it forward and then obediently perch on it as I waited to hear what must surely be bad news, conveyed as it was to me by the police early on a Sunday morning.

'I'm sorry, but I have to tell you . . . there has been an accident. I'm afraid your aunt is dead.'

'What do you mean? She can't be. I only saw her last night — I had dinner with her!' I protested, as if that had given Grace Arbuthnot divine protection. Even in that dreadful moment I realized that if I said this aloud the policewoman would think I was making a pun in very bad taste on my own name.

'Then you may have been the last person to see her alive. Can you tell me something about your evening? Where did you have dinner? What time did you part company?'

'We met at the Golden Pheasant ... ' I started to tell her, then as the full import of the policewoman's words sank in, 'What has happened to her? Did she have an accident on the way home?'

The policewoman shook her head, 'No, not on the way home — and it wasn't a car accident.'

'Then what — what did happen?' I demanded, bringing my hand down on the bar top as I spoke, 'There was nothing wrong with her when I left the restaurant; she was fine — just fine. In fact she was in great form all evening. We had a wonderful time. I just don't believe it.' I looked into the other woman's eyes and saw the sympathy there and knew she was speaking the truth. For a moment I couldn't speak, then, in a voice I hardly recognized as my own, I whispered, 'What happened? Tell me how she died.'

'She was found dead in her car, early this morning,' the policewoman told me in a quiet voice.

'You mean she had a heart attack or something?' I questioned, my voice fading out on the last word as reasons for sudden death

3

other than a heart attack filled my mind.

The policewoman shook her head. 'She died from a blow to the head.'

'She had a heart attack and fell?' I croaked, desperate to learn that it was my aunt's heart that had killed her, not any of the many other possibilities that swam through my mind.

The policewoman again shook her head slowly. 'Look, isn't there anywhere more . . . well, more comfortable you could sit?' I was leaning rather than sitting on the pine stool. I looked vaguely towards the more comfortable chairs; she took my arm and led me into the living area where she pushed me gently but firmly into the nearest armchair. 'Put your head down,' she instructed. 'I'll make you a cup of tea.' I realized afterwards that she must have thought I was going to faint or, worse, throw up. She gave the back of my head a firm push before turning back to the kitchen area where she soon had the electric jug heating. I heard cupboard doors opening and closing but I didn't have the energy to direct her. She was probably used to finding things in strange kitchens, for, by the time the water boiled she had a teabag in a mug, milk out of the fridge and was spooning sugar liberally out of a bag. Strong, hot and very sweet tea was obviously what she considered the best antidote for shock.

She put the mug into my hand and simply ignored my weak protest that I didn't take that much sugar.

'Drink this.' she said firmly. Only when she saw the cup was to my lips and that I was carefully sipping the hot tea did she add quietly, 'She was sitting in the driver's seat, slumped over the wheel, but it was not a heart attack. Something — someone — had hit her on the back of the head.'

'You mean she was killed deliberately? Murdered? No! Oh no, I can't believe it!' My voice rose sharply from a sibilant whisper to something approaching a shriek as I put the mug down on the small table at my side and clapped one hand over my mouth in a childish gesture, suddenly afraid I might actually vomit. With a supreme effort of will I gained a measure of control, slowly lowered my hand and pleaded, 'It can't be true. Tell me it isn't true.'

'I'm afraid there really isn't any doubt that she was murdered. Try and drink your tea — please,' she added after a pause.

Obediently I picked up the mug again and managed another sip. 'But who would do such a thing; who would *want* to do such a thing? To Aunt Grace, of all people?' I sipped slowly at the tea for a few moments before asking in a voice that broke as I formed the question, 'Who . . . who found her?'

'The next-door neighbour, John Bowles. He came home late, or very early this morning, and was alerted that something was wrong by your aunt's dog, which was barking persistently. At first Mr Bowles thought he was barking at him, but when the dog kept it up, even after Mr Bowles had parked his own car and gone indoors, he thought maybe he should investigate. That was when he found her. Now . . . ' — the woman was suddenly all briskness and efficiency — 'as you are apparently the last person to have seen her alive, perhaps you could get dressed and come along with me?'

'Yes — yes of course.' I felt numb, from my brain to my toes. This surely was a nightmare: they couldn't be arresting me for Grace's murder?

When I made no move but simply stared at the policewoman she must have guessed my thoughts, for the woman inside the uniform reasserted herself. She smiled reassuringly and said, in a much softer tone, 'Finish your tea — then get dressed; I'll wait for you.'

I nodded and slowly drained the large mug of tea which I found, in spite of, or perhaps because of, its sweetness surprisingly restorative. I moved about my bedroom in a haze collecting clothes from closet and drawers. I returned to the kitchen in jeans and sweatshirt. My hair was brushed, but I had not bothered to apply any make-up. My mug had been refilled in my absence and I reached gratefully across the bar top as it was pushed towards me by the kindly policewoman.

'May I make a phone call?' I asked, grasping the warm mug gratefully between both hands.

'But of course. You aren't under arrest, you know.'

I responded with a thin smile of relief as I reached over and picked up the phone. I punched in Malcolm's number, hesitating slightly, even though it was one I knew almost as well as my own. He was a long time answering and when he did he didn't disguise the yawn in his voice.

'Hi. Happy — ' he began. I cut him short.

'Malcolm, something dreadful — quite awful — has happened . . . ' I took a deep breath to control the quaver in my voice. 'My aunt has been . . . murdered.' I needed another breath before I could even say the word. 'There is a policewoman here now. I have to go with her . . . ' I remembered I was supposed to be meeting him for lunch. 'I don't think I will be able to — '

'I'll be right there!' he told me. I looked at the phone in my hand. It was now burbling with the dialling tone. Malcolm was coming and he would, I knew, take charge. He was good at that, and this time I was grateful, quite forgetting the number of times I had chafed at what I had considered his high-handed manner. Slowly I replaced the phone in its cradle and turned round to face the policewoman.

'My . . . a friend,' I told her, choosing for some reason the ambiguous label rather than the word 'boyfriend'. 'He is coming straight here.'

The policewoman, relieved to see that the tea, or the phone call, or both, appeared to have restored me somewhat, nodded and picked up her keys from the breakfast bar, where she had dropped them when she made the tea. 'Perhaps you could go straight to your aunt's place when your . . . friend gets here.'

* ★ ★

I almost fell into Malcolm's arms when he arrived a short while after the policewoman had left. 'Oh . . . ' My voice cracked on a sob. 'Thank you for coming. It's so awful, I don't seem able to believe it just yet. It seems — it seems as if she has been . . . murdered.' My voice died away on the last word as I clung to Malcolm in desperate gratitude.

8

'Poor old girl!' he said, as he patted me on the back. I wasn't sure whether he was referring to me or my aunt. 'What a thing to happen on your birthday!'

I stepped back slightly and stared at him. 'It isn't Aunt Grace's fault,' I wailed. 'She didn't get murdered deliberately!'

'No, no of course not — I didn't mean . . . Well, perhaps we had better get going. Do we have to go to the police station?'

I shook my head. 'No — to her — to Grace's place. Oh, Malcolm,' — my hand shot up to my mouth once more as the shocking and terrifying thought struck me — 'will I have to identify the . . . her?'

When we arrived at Grace Arbuthnot's flat over her antiques shop, I could hear Billy's frenzied barking, now sounding a hoarse note of desperation. 'Poor dog,' I exclaimed. 'Hasn't anyone let him out?'

'Apparently not.' Malcolm's tone was dry and from the expression on his face I could see that poor Billy's incarceration was not causing him undue concern.

'I must let him out,' I said. I unlocked the back door, which opened on to a small vestibule and a flight of stairs to the flat over the shop. I used the key I knew my aunt kept under the shoe-scraper. Watching Billy as, with a perfunctory wag of his tail, he dashed past me to relieve himself in the back yard, I observed out of the corner of my eye two police officers: the woman I had already met and a man who I later learned, was a detective sergeant, watching me thoughtfully. I shut the yard gate, leaving the dog outside the flat, and returned to the drive running alongside the house to join Malcolm, who was standing a little apart from the police presence. 'I'm so sorry, but I just had to let the poor old boy out,' I explained.

'I see you know where your aunt kept the key.' I thought I caught a quick glance flash between the detective and the policewoman but I was busy rummaging in my bag and couldn't be sure.

'I have my own key actually,' I said defensively. 'I insisted I had a set; shop keys as well — for emergencies. I . . . ' My voice faded and I choked back a sob. Neither I nor Grace had ever envisaged an emergency like this one.

'You visited your aunt pretty regularly?' the detective asked after a brief pause which had given me a moment or two to collect myself.

'Oh yes, I was round here a lot. I helped out in the shop from time to time too, weekends and so on if she needed to go away, or, if she was out or anything, I looked after Billy.'

'You would be pretty familiar then with the interior?'

'The interior? Oh, yes,' I assured him, not quite sure what he was getting at.

'I think he means — ' Malcolm began, but the detective cut him short.

'Good. We would just like you to take a look round and see if anything is missing.'

'But of course.' I tried to keep the quaver out of my voice, reminding myself that looking round the flat would not be nearly as bad as having to identify my aunt. I took a deep breath and followed the detective towards the door; the policewoman followed me and Malcolm brought up the rear. For one wild panic-stricken moment I wanted to escape — make a run for it — but I knew that would be difficult if not downright impossible, flanked as I was by the law.

Billy joined the sad little procession as we made our way single file up the stairs, although 'joined' was probably not quite the right word. When he saw where we were going he bounded past the ascending feet till he was actually in the lead. I noticed the policewoman smiled slightly, but across the faces of both men flitted a curiously similar expression of irritation, almost of annoyance.

There seemed to be nothing out of place. Dishes were washed and draining on the counter, the bed was made and obviously not recently slept in.

'It looks just the same as always,' I mumbled, fighting back tears. 'Grace — my aunt — was always a neat, methodical sort of person. She always left things tidy.' Even as I spoke I noticed two glasses, whisky tumblers, side by side on the left-hand draining-board. They had obviously been used but not washed; that in itself was odd.

The detective also saw them. 'Your aunt was a whisky drinker?'

'Yes — no — well, that is, she sometimes liked a nightcap before she went to bed — for medicinal reasons she always said . . . but — '

'But not earlier in the day?'

'Well, no. And it is very unlike her to leave them on the draining-board unwashed. She was very fussy like that and always rinsed things immediately.'

'Maybe she was running late — you say she met you for dinner last night?'

'Yes — yes, she did. And you are probably right — she was running late and didn't have time to do anything with them. All the same . . . '

'It was unusual for her to leave them like that, is that what you were about to say, Miss Divine?'

'Yes. I was also wondering — '

12

'You are wondering who she was drinking whisky with just before she came to meet you. Is that so?'

'Well, yes, it is. To tell you the truth I have never known her drink whisky with anyone before. It was — well, I suppose it was her secret small vice. She just liked her little tipple sometimes before she went to bed. Probably me, and Billy of course, were the only people who knew about it.'

I saw the detective's brow crease in a slight frown and his lips tightened. I got the impression that he thought I was making light of the situation — even perhaps taking the mickey out of him, by referring to a mere dog in such a manner. I was about to apologize but catching the policewoman's eye and detecting a definite glint of sympathy, laced with amusement, I changed my mind. What I had said was the truth, anyway.

I glanced round the room. As far as I could see everything was normal, neat and tidy with a faint hint of lavender polish hanging on the air. Just as I had known it for almost as long as I had known my aunt Grace. Then something quite trivial caught my eye; a tiny bit of white paper sticking out of the front of the bureau in the corner of the room, I walked over and pulled down the sloping lid.

'Oh my goodness!' I exclaimed, feeling

even as I spoke that my words were totally inadequate. Instead of being neatly stacked into the pigeonholes papers were pushed in at random, even screwed up in some cases, Never in the whole of her orderly existence would Grace Arbuthnot have left her bureau in such a state, or allowed it to get like that in the first place.

In one swift stride the two police officers flanked me. 'Please do not touch anything, Miss Divine.' The detective's voice was crisp and authoritative.

'Someone has been in here. I've told you my aunt was a very tidy and orderly person; she would never, ever have left it like this.' I turned to the police officers. 'I have never seen her bureau look like this before,' I repeated. 'She always kept it locked, so I didn't often see inside, but whenever I did it was always tidy — a place for everything and everything in its place. That was her motto.'

'You tell me she kept it locked, yet you went straight to it and opened it without a key a few moments ago. Did you know it was unlocked?'

I looked up and met the detective's pale-grey eyes, hard and accusing, and I immediately felt guilty, although I couldn't have said why.

'I suppose I must have done.' I shrugged and wondered how I had known. I looked him in the eye and firmly crushed down my absurd feeling of guilt for some crime I knew I had not committed. 'It was that bit of paper sticking out — I think it was jamming the lid open. Someone must have rammed it shut in a hurry.' I knew I was gabbling and the tiny lift to one of the detective's eyebrows did nothing to calm me. 'Seeing that, I suppose I just acted without thinking.'

'Quite,' the detective muttered, confirming my fear that he suspected me of — but no, he couldn't. After a pause, he continued, 'Would you have any idea what whoever it was, was looking for?'

I shook my head. 'None at all. I don't really know what she kept there; I always assumed it was bills — that sort of thing.' I looked desperately from one police officer to the other, their silence stabbing me as if they had accused me out loud. 'You can't think I had anything to do with this. I loved my aunt. I would never, ever do — have never done — anything to hurt her.' Conscious of the rising hysteria in my voice I turned desperately to Malcolm. 'You know I did love — you know I wouldn't . . . ' My voice broke on a sob. The thought that anyone could imagine I could have anything to do with my aunt's death added an unbearable load to my shock and grief.

15

The woman stepped forward and laid a hand on my arm. 'Calm yourself. No one thinks anything of the sort; we are just hoping you can shed some light on things — perhaps give us a clue. If we knew what whoever it was, was searching for that would be a help.'

I choked back my sobs and rising hysteria and looked at those two glasses.

'If you have finished with Miss Divine then I think I should take her home,' Malcolm told the police officers. I wasn't sure I liked being spoken of in the third person, as if I wasn't really there. 'That is unless you need me to . . . er . . . '

'We have been contacted by a man who claims to be Miss Arbuthnot's stepson. If he can identify her then we will contact you, Miss Divine, when we need to talk to you again.'

I took a deep breath, partly of relief that they didn't need me any more at the moment and partly to restore my swirling sense of equilibrium, which felt as if it were spiralling out of control. It was only when Malcolm was getting into the car that it hit me.

'Malcolm!' I exclaimed, my voice strident. 'Aunt Grace didn't have a stepson!'

16

2

I stared at Malcolm in horror. 'I tell you, there is no stepson!' I all but yelled at him.

'Get in the car and I'll take you home; you are distraught. The police have obviously been in touch with him.'

'I am sure.' But there was a waver in my voice. Malcolm was firmly pushing me towards the passenger seat of his car when I remembered Grace's little dog.

'Billy!' I resisted his efforts and turned to face him.

'Is that his name?' Malcolm asked. 'I told you that if the police said they had been in touch with your aunt's stepson then she must have one. You must have forgotten — shock affects people like that.'

'Billy is her dog!' I screeched in his face. 'I can't leave him here. Grace loved him; he was family to her.'

'Don't worry about the dog.' Malcolm told me in the same patronizing voice. 'I am sure the police will deal with him.'

'Deal with him?' I stared at him, my distraught mind grappling with horrific thoughts about just how the police might choose to do that. 'I'll get him — we can take him with us.'

'Don't be silly, Angie. Let the police cope with him. They'll take him to a shelter, the RSPCA or something. Or maybe the stepson will take him.'

'You still don't believe me, do you? Aunt Grace did not have a stepson, but she did have a dog and I am taking Billy back with me.' With a vigorous shrug I freed myself from his restraining hands and ran back to the dog who, to my relief, was trotting towards me. I swept him up in my arms and, still clasping him, clambered into the front seat of Malcolm's car.

'Couldn't you — er — put him in the boot?'

'No I could not! How could you even suggest it? He is like me — upset. I'll hold him in my arms then he won't touch any part of your precious car!' I glared at Malcolm who accepted the situation with a sigh and pushed the key into the ignition.

Noting his scowl I wanted to tell him that neither the dog nor I smelt so he could take that expression off his face. Instead, I held the little dog even more tightly and wondered what had happened to my feelings for Malcolm. Only yesterday evening I had confided in Grace that if Malcolm asked me to marry him, I would consider saying 'Yes'. I remembered now that she had been reserved in her reaction, telling me not to rush into anything. I felt that if she could see his reaction to poor Billy she would have been more explicit.

As Malcolm turned the key and the engine sprang to life another car drew up and a young man leaped out even before it stopped. 'Are you — ?' he began, his hands clutching the glass of the half-open window at my side, but, before he could say more, Malcolm had pressed the button that closed it and he was forced to move his fingers before they were trapped and to step back quickly.

'Bloody reporters!' Malcolm gritted, as the car jerked forward. 'They are like vultures.'

I half-turned in my seat and caught a glimpse of the young man staring after us with an expression I could not quite fathom on his face. Malcolm, I thought, was in a foul mood and I regretted that I was committed to having lunch with him.

'You can leave the dog in the garden, can't you?' Malcolm suggested, as he drew up outside my flat.

'No.' I tightened my arms round the little dog, gaining some comfort from the small hairy body. 'I'll keep him with me. He is upset and someone might let him out.' Billy licked my chin, I found it comforting but Malcolm gave a slight shudder.

'Thank you for bringing me home,' I said politely, hoping he would go. My hopes were dashed when he got out of the car.

'I'll see you in. We could both — I think — do with a restorative.'

'Yes. I'll make some coffee,' I told him, adding, 'Have you had any breakfast?' As I asked the question I remembered that I hadn't, then felt a twinge of guilt at the thought; I shouldn't be thinking about food — not now — when Grace . . .

Malcolm followed me indoors. 'Thank you — we need something,' he agreed. I made a pot of strong coffee, prepared toast, and put out a jar of honey. I was surprised that I could eat anything and still felt a trifle guilty that I could.

'I still can't believe Grace is really dead,' I ruminated, through a mouthful of toast. 'She was fine when I saw her last night. She took me out to dinner — a birthday treat. Mind you,'

I added reflectively, 'I did think once or twice that she was a bit — how shall I say — a bit *distraite*. Once or twice she seemed to go off into her own thoughts and I got the impression she wasn't really listening to me.'

'We all do that at times,' Malcolm pointed out.

'Oh I know, but I felt as if her mind was somewhere else.'

'You're thinking that now because you know what happened to her. Are you sure you thought it at the time?' Malcolm asked, reasonably enough.

I shook my head. Truthfully, I wasn't entirely sure, and of course he was quite right, everybody did this at times. I sighed and picked up my coffee mug. I had made the brew so strong that the spoon could almost stand up in it but it certainly did make me feel better.

'We'll go out and have a good lunch — for your birthday. Sitting here brooding won't do you any good and it certainly won't help Grace.' Brisk and sensible; he was, I told myself, just being kind.

'All right,' I agreed somewhat ungraciously. 'I expect you are right. But suppose — you don't think the police will want to see me again?'

'Not this soon. You gave them all the help you could, checked that nothing seemed to be missing or broken. If they want to know anything else I expect they will get on to her stepson.'

'Malcolm,' I gritted, 'I've told you — Grace did not have a stepson. She never married.'

'Are you sure she never married? After all,

21

you hadn't known her all her life, or even all your life.'

'I'm sure she never married and even more sure she didn't have a stepson. I would have known.' I spoke more confidently than I felt; in the back of my mind there was a niggling thought that maybe I didn't really know all there was to know about Grace's life before she had brought me into it.

Malcolm suggested I should have a rest and he would pick me up later and take me out to lunch. I nodded, somewhat absently. I didn't particularly want to rest, I wanted to think but, aware that I could do neither with Malcolm standing over me, I yawned and murmured, 'Good idea,' trying to hide my relief at the prospect of a short spell alone to recoup my shattered senses. With a rather childish gesture I rubbed my eyes to underline the yawn.

'You look washed out,' he remarked.

'Oh, thanks. Just what a girl wants to hear on her birthday.'

'Perhaps it would be better if you had a good rest today and we went out for an early dinner?' Malcolm suggested, ignoring my tart comment.

The idea of a good rest — just flaking out — appealed. 'I think that's probably a good idea.' I stifled yet another prodigious yawn, wondering if I was overdoing it.

'I'll pop the dog out in the garden as I leave.' Malcolm got up to go and moved towards Billy.

'You will do no such thing. I've told you, that poor little dog has, like me, suffered trauma. You will leave him inside with me; we will comfort one another.'

It was obvious from his expression that Malcolm did not appreciate this little speech. He shrugged, and promised to be back by six o'clock to take me out to dinner. He moved to the door where he paused, then turned back into the room. 'Be sensible. Try to stop thinking about it — have a rest,' he advised. He closed the door carefully and quietly, as if I were already asleep and he was afraid of waking me.

Tired though I was I found it hard to rest. 'Something is wrong about this business,' I told Billy. 'Well, of course it is. Grace is dead, what could be wronger than that?' I was beyond worrying about the niceties of grammar. I looked earnestly into the anxious face of the little dog. 'Did you know she had a stepson?' He put his head on one side and looked at me. 'No, of course you didn't, any more than I did. So if there is no stepson why do the police think there is?'

The answer to this seemed alarmingly

obvious: they thought there was because someone had claimed to be so. But who? And why should he make an appearance now, of all times, when my aunt had just been brutally murdered? Was it a bizarre coincidence, or were the two events connected? With a deep sigh I leaned back among the cushions on the sofa and closed my eyes. My mind might be whirling but my body was exhausted. I felt Billy jump up beside me and drop his head on to my lap. I ran my fingers through his silky coat, finding comfort in his presence and the knowledge that he shared my shock and grief. My body relaxed and by the time Billy's small frame heaved with a sigh of relief at finding someone both to comfort and to offer comfort to, I was asleep.

*   *   *

It was Billy who woke me two hours later; he was standing at the door whining. Sighing I pulled myself to my feet and went to let him out into my small patio garden. At least that was what I called it; most people referred to it as a yard. As soon as the door was open the little dog shot past me, his shrill and urgent bark reverberating in my skull. Following his progress with my eyes, I saw that he was at the high wooden fence. Looking over it was a man.

'Quiet, Billy,' I admonished somewhat half-heartedly, for in truth I was feeling like protesting myself; in my fraught state after the appalling news about my aunt I felt that my privacy, even my safety, were being threatened and I would have liked to voice my feelings as vociferously as Billy. I stared at the man; there was something familiar about him. I had a good memory for faces and I instantly placed him as the reporter who had tried to talk to me when Malcolm was driving away from my aunt's place. Anger flared: how dared he follow me — and what on earth was he doing in the next door garden?

'I've absolutely nothing to say to you.' My voice was cold. 'How dare you follow me. Please go home.'

'I am home.' His lopsided grin which, had I been in a different mood, I might have found attractive, merely irritated me. 'I — we've just moved in.'

'We?' In spite of myself I could not resist asking the question.

'Jimmy and me. He is six.'

'Oh.' The monosyllable hung in the air, accusing and disbelieving. It was a weekend so he would not be at school, but there was no sign of a child.

'My nephew is spending the day with a friend while I get straight — well, sort of,' he ended on a rueful note. 'I have to babysit tomorrow.'

'I see,' I said, more because some sort of response was expected of me than because I did. We stared at one another for a few rather difficult moments before he said, 'I'd better get on or Jimmy will be back before I have done anything. Nice to have met you.'

Even though I didn't believe him I felt guilty. Reporter or not, as a new neighbour he deserved ordinary civility at the very least. 'If there is anything I can do . . . ' I began tentatively. But he was gone and I was left talking to the fence. Billy looked up at me and wagged his tail; I felt he was taking credit for driving off an unwelcome intruder.

I went back inside and made myself a cup of tea, which I sipped thoughtfully. I still hadn't come to terms with what had happened to my aunt — would I ever? I dismissed the idea of Grace having a stepson, or I would have dismissed it if the memory of the police and their absolute certainty that he existed hadn't resurfaced. Surely I would have known if it had been true? On that conviction I allowed myself to wonder about my new neighbour; the very last thing I wanted was the flapping ears and prying eyes of a reporter next door. Actually, I mused, his eyes had been rather nice, a sort of warm hazel, soft and kind. I pulled myself up sharply; if anything was soft I was. I looked down at the little dog — now *his* eyes were warm and kind. He looked up into my face and wagged his tail.

'All the same, Billy,' I told him, 'I don't know that I like the idea of a reporter next door — in the circumstances.'

Noticing the dog looking at me appealingly with his head cocked on one side I guessed he might be hungry. Well, I hadn't any dog food in the house so he would have to make do with whatever I could find. That proved to be a crust from the end of the loaf and the dregs from the milk carton.

'I'm sorry, but that is the best I can do,' I told him apologetically. 'I'll go shopping for both of us tomorrow. In the meantime you will have to stay here this evening and look after things for me because I have to go out.' I rinsed my teacup and headed for the shower.

★ ★ ★

Malcolm arrived a few minutes before six. Billy greeted him loudly. 'Shut up!' he shouted back.

'There's no need to yell at him,' I remonstrated, as I appeared in the room looking, as Malcolm hastily told me, much better. 'He is only doing his duty — telling me you have arrived,' I added reproachfully. 'See, he is quiet now. Yes, I should look better: I've worked hard on it. It's wonderful what make-up can hide.' I walked to the mirror over the mantelpiece to fix my ear-rings.

'Don't bother with those,' Malcolm told me. 'I've got your birthday present here.' He handed me a small gift-wrapped parcel, obviously from the size and shape a jeweller's box. I opened it, suddenly convinced it was a ring and hoping it was not.

'Oh — how lovely!' I exclaimed with genuine pleasure as I drew out one of a pair of exquisite earrings. Shaped like tear drops, they caught the light and flashed small rainbows. They looked like diamonds but I knew they could not be; diamonds this size would be worth almost as much as the Koh-i-noor.

'They are quartz crystal,' Malcolm told me, 'not glass. Put them on.'

Obediently I turned back to the mirror and hooked them carefully into my ear lobes. 'They are beautiful, Malcolm. Thank you very much,' I told him with genuine delight. I turned to him with a smile and picking up my bag moved to the door, my spirits lifting at the prospect of an evening out.

'What about . . . him?' Malcolm asked, nodding towards Billy.

I looked at him in surprise; surely he wasn't suggesting we should take the dog with us.

'I mean, aren't you going to put him out?'

'Put him out?' I repeated in the tone of voice I might well have used if he had said put him to sleep. 'Of course not. I am leaving him in here.'

'But surely — I mean, didn't your aunt put him outside when she went out?'

'No, she did not. If you remember he was shut inside when we got to her place. He stays in. I should never forgive myself if anything happened to him.' My voice cracked. Malcolm shrugged and moved to the door. I could see he thought I was far too emotional about the animal.

Settling in the passenger seat beside Malcolm I did my best to put the appalling events of the last twenty-four hours out of my mind. It was not easy and I had to ask Malcolm to repeat things more than once. When I sat staring at the menu in the very classy restaurant he had chosen he recalled me to the present in a voice that had a distinct edge to it.

'Well . . . what do you fancy?'

Hastily I brought my attention back to the menu I was holding up in front of myself and did my best to whip up enthusiasm for at least one of the many tasty dishes. Malcolm beckoned the wine waiter and ordered half a bottle of champagne without consulting me. In my horror over the death of my aunt I had temporarily forgotten that today was actually my own birthday. As I raised my glass to my lips I murmured sardonically, 'When the chips are down, order champagne.'

'I ordered it to celebrate your birthday. But if it helps to raise your spirits I am pleased.' I thought Malcolm sounded stuffy. Even more so when he added, 'That — if I may say so — is rather a silly saying.'

I wanted to tell him he may not say so but merely raised my glass to him in response to his 'Happy birthday!'

We had reached the coffee stage when I, who had worked hard to keep my mind in the present and my conversation off the immediate past, gave in to a yawn. God, but I was whacked. 'I still can't understand all that about Aunt Grace's stepson.' The words were out before I could stop them.

Malcolm frowned but managed to control his irritation. 'Stop thinking about it. If the police say she had a stepson then I'm willing to bet they are correct. Be thankful.'

'Thankful?'

'Well, it let you off the hook.'

'You mean I would — I would have had to identify her?' My voice dropped to a sibilant hiss at the thought. Yes, indeed I supposed I had something to be thankful for. Yet . . . 'All the same it seems odd that he should turn up now just when she — when she . . . ' My voice trailed away; I still couldn't bring myself to actually say aloud that my aunt was dead. In some strange superstitious way I felt that by not admitting the fact it might not be true.

'An odd coincidence, I admit.'

'Yes, I expect that is all it is.' I forbore to add that I didn't believe in coincidences, which usually turned out to be connections instead.

'You look all in,' Malcolm told me as he drained his coffee cup and set it down in its saucer.

'Yes, I am,' I admitted. 'I can't say it has been the best birthday I have ever had.'

'I'll take you home.' He turned to catch the waiter's eye and snapped his fingers for the bill. I had always rather admired the way he did this; tonight for some reason it irritated me. Looking across the table at him I tried to revive the feelings that only the previous

31

evening had made me confide in my aunt that if he asked me I would marry him. Why did I feel differently tonight — where had that feeling gone? I couldn't honestly blame Malcolm; he had been considerate, thoughtful, and even kind — in his own way. Perhaps tomorrow after a good night's sleep I would recapture my feeling for him. I suppressed the thought that I wasn't sure I wanted to.

'I won't come in,' Malcolm told me, as he watched me fumble in my bag for my key. 'Not tonight. I can see you really are worn out. I know it has been a very stressful day.' He leaned forward and kissed me gently, obviously without expecting anything from me. For a moment I was touched and felt a rush of my old feeling for him, or was it guilt? Then he spoilt it by adding, 'Try and put the whole business out of your mind; you weren't really that close to her, it wasn't as if she were your mother.'

I moved away from him and, having found my key, inserted it in the lock and turned it swiftly and decisively. How did he know how close I had been to Aunt Grace, who was, after all, my only living relative?

'Thank you, Malcolm, for a lovely evening, and for your present . . . ' Automatically one hand went to my ear and touched the pendant. 'You really have been kind and helpful and I'm sorry I've been such a wet blanket.' I leaned forward and planted a light kiss on his cheek, then with a sigh of relief I escaped into my own tiny flat. As I reached for the light switch there was a thump from the lounge.

3

'Billy!' I cried in relief as he ran to greet me. I had temporarily forgotten that I had a house-guest. The 'thump' I had heard must have been him landing on the floor from the couch. 'Come on, you had better go out before we go to bed,' I told him, as I let him out into the tiny patio garden. Afraid to lose him — though how I could I didn't know — I waited till he was ready to come in.

Feeling drained of all energy I expected to drop off to sleep the minute my head hit the pillow but my active mind had very different ideas. No, I was quite sure Grace had no stepson. I had known her for so long I could not have missed knowing such an important fact about my aunt.

My thoughts travelled back in time to my first meeting with Grace. She had seemed old then, and daunting; now, fifteen years later, she did not seem to have aged at all and was not in the least daunting. My breath caught in my throat in a sound midway between a gasp and a sob as I realized that I was thinking in the present. As if she were still alive. I just could not bring myself to think of her as dead, on a slab in a mortuary. Not Grace, who had come to mean everything to me over the years.

*　*　*

I had been just eight years old; in fact it was my birthday. God, was every life-changing event that happened destined to occur on my birthday? Because it was my birthday I had not been alarmed by the summons to the headmistress's study. On the contrary, I had happily anticipated something good; a present from my parents perhaps, or even a message. The hope had even sparked that my parents themselves had turned up as a surprise. In my heart I knew that that was most unlikely, as they were in India working as medical missionaries and unless I was invited to another pupil's home for the holidays I was destined to spend them at the school with the handful of other children whose parents were overseas and couldn't make arrangements for their children for the holidays.

I remembered tapping on the door, waiting for the crisp 'Enter!' from Miss Deakin and the inexplicable feeling of foreboding when I saw the tall, grey-haired woman, smartly but severely dressed in much the same style as the headmistress, who immediately jumped to

35

her feet when I walked into the room.

'This is Angela,' Miss Deakin told her but then left the visitor to introduce herself.

The strange woman stared at me for a moment.

'Hello, Angela. My name is Grace, I am your aunt.' In a well-modulated voice she addressed me as if I were an adult. I didn't believe her. I had no aunts and uncles: both my parents were only children; I had no grandparents either because my mother's parents were both dead and my father never had any. He was an orphan. I looked the strange woman in the eye and shook my head. 'I haven't got any aunts — or uncles.' For a second I thought the stranger looked as if she might burst into tears. Much later on I learned that my mother had cut her only sister out of her life. I could not understand such a cruel action. Even as a child I could see kindness in the visitor's face, she was looking at me as if she thought I were the one hurt. We stared at one another in some sort of recognition and acceptance, until Miss Deakin's crisp voice broke the silence.

'Miss Arbuthnot has come to take you home with her because — well, I am afraid she has some sad news for you . . . ' Her voice faded out and, murmuring, 'I'll arrange for

Matron to put her things together,' she left the room.

I went on staring in silence, but I did not back away from the hand held out towards me.

'I am your aunt, I promise you. Your mother was my sister.'

All my senses were alert at her use of the past tense, so I muttered ungraciously: 'I don't want to go with you. I don't know you.'

The woman sighed and let my hand drop in a gesture of helplessness. 'I really am your aunt, Angela. I have come to take you home with me.'

There was no comfort in her words and I repeated sullenly: 'I don't want to go with you. I have to stay here till Mummy and Daddy come for me; they told me so.'

'Oh, Angela . . . ' I looked up and saw that the strange woman who said she was my aunt had tears glistening in her eyes. This frightened and embarrassed me. I looked down, shuffled my feet and waited for her to leave. When she did she took me with her.

★　★　★

Lying sleepless in bed, doing my best to come to terms with my aunt's death, I recalled with something like shame the frightened and sulky child who had insisted that Grace was nothing to do with her. It had taken the combined efforts of Grace and the headmistress as well as the matron to persuade me to leave the school with her.

Eventually I had come to terms with the death of my parents and accepted the fact that Grace was the only family I had. From acceptance had gradually grown affection and then love. Now, looking back, I knew I had every reason to be grateful too.

My parents had left me what little money they had and this Grace had invested wisely so that over the next ten years it had grown into a tidy little nest egg, sufficient for me to continue my education after leaving school. Now at twenty-three I had a not very good history degree, which I had only used for long enough to convince me that teaching was not my *métier*, and a passionate love of books and reading which I owed more to my aunt's upbringing than my college education. Fortunately Grace had seen that putting me into a classroom as a teacher was tantamount to trying to hammer a square peg into a round hole and had suggested a course in computer skills and bookkeeping.

After graduating from the twelve-month course I went back to Belmeade, not to live with Grace permanently, or even work in her antiques business. I would have liked that, but she said there was not enough work to support us both. With my passion for books I was delighted to land a job in a bookshop and when Grace offered me a small flat she normally leased to students she agreed with me that as we were both independent people, we would remain better friends if we did not share a home. But that did not mean that I did not see a good deal of my aunt.

Tom Ensley was a mine of information about antiquarian books, but he had never learned to master computers. I soon learned a good deal about the book trade and revolutionized the office side of the business. I had also met people, including Malcolm who was a regular at the shop, although, if my memory served me right, he very seldom, if ever, purchased any books. My relationship with Grace moved on to a new footing, adult to adult instead of adult to child, I grew to love her all over again and considered her my best friend. Beneath her austere and some-what autocratic exterior lurked a keen mind and a warm heart. Remembering just a few of the many kindnesses I had experienced since she first rescued me from boarding-school the realization that she was no longer part of my life overwhelmed me. I pulled the sheet over my head, buried my face in the pillow and allowed the tears to flow unchecked.

When I felt a weight on the bed I stiffened in fear, then a cold wet nose was poked under the sheet. How many times would Billy scare the wits out of me before I remembered he now lived with me? I drew a measure of comfort from his presence and the memory of the support Malcolm had offered me today. I felt a small prick of guilt that I had been such a poor companion. One thing I was quite sure about: whatever Malcolm and the police claimed, Grace had not had a stepson.

I reached out and put an arm round the little dog; he too must be feeling grief in his doggy way. I spite of my misery it amused me to imagine Malcolm's horror if he could see me sharing my bed with Billy.

Now that he had intruded into my mind I found it hard to banish Malcolm. I had let Grace think that I might consider a permanent relationship with him and her reaction had been, to say the least, unenthusiastic. I regretted this exchange now that it was too late to correct it. I enjoyed Malcolm's company well enough but could not now consider a permanent relationship with him. He was at least twelve years older than me for starters, and his attitude to Billy had grated. Now that it was too late I wished I could discuss him with Grace and find out what it was she disliked about him.

Feeling as young and insecure as on that terrible day when Grace came to fetch me from school and I learned that both my parents were dead, I felt the body of the little dog curled up on the bed and derived comfort from his presence. This, I thought, had been one helluva birthday.

I didn't realize what the noise was when the alarm roused me from a terrifying scene: flames licked round the building that contained Grace's flat and shop and a fire truck, with clanging bell, was just arriving. Still half in my dream I reached out automatically and pressed the button on my bedside clock. As the noise stopped I came fully awake and remembered with horror the events of the previous day.

I padded to the door and let Billy out while I showered and dressed. Feeling less as if I had been pulled through a wringer but still heavy with grief I went into the kitchen to make myself much needed coffee. As I spooned instant granules into a mug and dropped a piece of bread into the toaster I remembered Billy, surprised that he hadn't already demanded admittance. The reason was obvious as soon as I stepped outside.

The face and shoulders of a small boy were

visible over the top of the fence. Obviously he was standing on something. He was watching Billy, who was pushing a large red ball around with his nose, getting ever more excited as the child screamed with laughter and cheered him on.

As I stepped through the door I heard a male voice call out, 'Jimmy — breakfast!' A few seconds later the face of the man I still thought of as 'that reporter' appeared next to that of the child. He was the first to speak;

'Good morning. I hope Jimmy didn't disturb you.'

'Not at all. I have been up for some time . . . ' I lied. 'I just came out to get the dog in.' I turned my attention to the ball; it was so large and red that I could not have missed it before, so the obvious conclusion was that the child had thrown it over.

The man followed my gaze. 'Sorry about that. Jimmy must have let it go over the fence.'

I sniffed. More like thrown it over deliberately, I thought. I moved across the tiny yard and picked up the ball. Billy looked at me, head cocked on one side, tail wagging. I managed to ignore the plea in his eyes and aimed the ball at the top of the fence. That is exactly what it hit, then it bounced back into my yard. Billy pounced on it with delight, the child shrieked with pleasure and the man barely suppressed a grin. Feeling foolish, I retrieved it and hurled it once more at the top of the fence. I hadn't aimed deliberately at the man's head, but he ducked and the ball disappeared from sight. With relief I turned my back and made for the door. When Billy didn't follow I was forced to turn back and call him. I was just in time to see two grinning faces disappear.

Drinking my coffee and thoughtfully spreading apricot jam on my slice of toast I considered the dog. I could hardly take him with me to the bookshop, though he would probably behave; Grace had often had him in her antiques shop. I could leave him out in the yard, but somehow the idea didn't appeal. Suppose something happened to him while I was away? Quite what I didn't clarify to myself. In the end I decided to leave him indoors and come back in my lunch hour to check that he was all right.

I let myself into the shop, surprised to find it not already open; my boss, Tom Ensley, was a stickler for punctuality in all things, including opening at, or before, the time it stated on the door. I checked my watch; I was actually five minutes late due to the business with the ball.

Tom was sitting on the high stool behind

the desk. It was his habitual perch, he claimed it gave him a bird's-eye view of the shop and even when he appeared to be busy with paperwork he certainly knew what was going on. This morning he was simply seated there, a vacant look on his face, his fading blue eyes gazing blankly at the shelves in front of him.

'Mr Ensley — what — are you all right?' Although he called me Angela, he had never suggested I call him by his Christian name. Now, when he didn't seem aware that I was there, I moved towards him and reaching out a tentative hand said, 'Tom?'

He started as if he had not been aware of my presence, then turned and looked at me. I was relieved to see the blank look fade from his eyes but when it was replaced by one of unbearable sadness I felt my own heart fill as memory of the previous day overwhelmed me.

'Good morning, Angie.' It was the first time he had used the diminutive, just as I had never used his Christian name before. 'You know — of course you do. She was related to you so you would have been told. It is so appalling I find it hard to believe yet . . . ' His voice faded away and I found myself waiting for his next words with my eyes on his face. He sighed and continued in so low a voice that I could scarcely hear the words . . . 'not entirely unexpected. I did warn her . . . '

I wanted to ask him what he meant, but with a slight shake — almost, I thought fancifully, as if he was shrugging himself back into his body, he sat up straight and turned towards me, his eyes now focused on me with their usual direct gaze. 'I have had a terrible shock, Angela, as I expect you have. I think, just this once, we should treat ourselves to a cup of tea before we begin the day's work.'

I correctly translated this as a request for me to go into the small kitchen at the rear of the shop and make tea for us both. Reflecting that my employer looked as if he were in a state of shock I spooned three spoonfuls of sugar into his mug instead of the one he usually took and added an extra one to my own. Stirring both mugs I carried them into the shop. Tom Ensley was still sitting at his desk. I placed the mug of well-sugared tea in front of him, murmuring something trite about drinking it while it was hot. He frequently got sidetracked by an interesting book or customer and never thought about his tea again. I was greatly relieved that the door remained shut and the shop was free of early-morning customers. We both, I felt, needed to get ourselves together before we faced the day and customers to the shop.

Tom, still staring blankly ahead, took a sip of his tea before musing in a low voice, trembling with emotion, 'I've known her such a long time. Before she settled here even, I was in love with her once.' His voice dropped away on the last words so that I wasn't entirely sure I heard them. I had to listen carefully to catch them.

'Then you would know . . . ' I wanted to ask about the stepson I was convinced did not exist — if he had known her so long . . . but while I was trying to frame the question in my mind he pulled himself together.

'Better open the shop,' he instructed, his tone devoid of expression. I turned to the door and saw a customer was waiting for me to turn the sign round and unlock the door. Even through the frosted glass the figure looked familiar. I gulped down the last of my tea and without hurrying moved to the door.

'Good morning. Again.' I emphasized the last word but didn't smile. 'What are you doing here?' I hissed under my breath. I had hoped to escape from some of yesterday's anguish when I came to work; the last thing I wanted was to be followed by a reporter.

He stepped past me into the shop. 'I came to look at books,' he told me, his raised eyebrows expressing wounded innocence. 'Or more precisely one particular book.' It was my turn to raise my eyebrows now, somewhat cynically. I didn't believe him, but asked civilly enough if I could help him. 'What was it you wanted?'

'Actually I am looking for a good copy of The Wind in the Willows, as it was first published, not a modern Disney thing but a genuine Kenneth Grahame.'

'I am sure you will find one if you look carefully among the children's books.' I indicated the children's shelves with a vague wave of my hand, then turned away to take our empty tea mugs to the kitchen. I slammed them down on the draining-board with unnecessary vigour, took a deep breath and walked back into the shop. What was it about this ... person ... that raised my hackles and made me behave in a manner that was quite unlike myself?

When he reappeared from the tall aisles of shelves carrying a book, I made an effort and forced a slight smile to my lips. Taking it from him and checking the price I exclaimed with genuine interest and pleasure, 'Ah yes. I had forgotten we had this — it is a very nice edition, I think. It is one of my favourite books — is it for your little boy?'

'Mine too — one of my favourites, I mean. But I seem to have mislaid my own copy. I thought I would read it to him when he goes to bed while he is staying with me.'

'He's not living with you permanently then? I thought . . . ' My voice faded as I recalled he had already explained to me that the boy was his nephew and he looked after him occasionally.

'Good gracious, No! In a quixotic moment of brotherly love I offered to have him overnight while my sister moves house and gets settled in.'

4

'Do you know what has happened to Grace's dog?' Tom called after my back as I moved towards the small office and the computer.

I turned, surprised by the question. 'Yes, he is staying with me. In fact I was going to ask you if you minded if I dashed home during the lunch hour to check on him. I left him shut inside, you see and he may want to — well, he may want to go out.'

'But of course — it is very good of you to look after him. I woke up in the night worrying about him. Grace was always so attached to him.' He gave a wry smile. 'I could never quite see why, but then there is no accounting for tastes.'

I permitted myself a small smile as I turned on the computer. I couldn't imagine Tom and Billy cohabiting happily and wondered idly why the little dog was so disliked by both Malcolm and Tom. It was lucky for him that I had taken him under my wing. Knowing how Grace had loved him it was, I felt, the least I could do and, to be honest, I was enjoying his company, or at least finding it a comfort.

The bell on the door summoned me into

the shop. I knew I could not rely on Tom to deal with customers if he happened to be engrossed in something else, such as a rare book catalogue; anyway I had done what needed to be done on the computer for the time being. I was grateful for the customers who demanded my attention; the last thing I wanted was time to think and remember what had happened to my aunt. When the shop emptied again I glanced at Tom. He was still absorbed in whatever it was that he was doing; I could see a pile of papers on his desk in front of him. I was well aware that he had known my aunt for a long time; in fact, I remembered him from my own childhood, but I had no idea how deep, or otherwise, their friendship went.

I remember her smiling when I told her I had applied for the post in his antiquarian bookshop. She muttered something about thinking I could do better, before remarking, somewhat tartly, that calling it that sounded better than a second-hand bookshop.

'It does indeed,' I remembered saying, adding, 'Problem is I don't know a thing about antiquarian books, Grace.' When I left school she had insisted that I stopped calling her Aunt or Auntie.

'That's no problem at all. Tom knows enough for a dozen people. But he is not so hot when it comes to running a business, or dealing with the general public and anything to do with computers are to him what Greek is to me.'

'Well, I am computer literate, but I have never run a business, nor have I had much to do with the general public and, as I said, though I love books and reading I don't know the first thing about antiquarian books.'

'Mainly he needs someone to keep his records and accounts straight, list his books on computer, that sort of thing. As for the public, well, I am sure sales will rocket when word gets around that there is a pretty girl instead of a crusty old man serving in the shop.'

I doubted that, but Grace turned out to be right; I had only been in the job six months when Tom Ensley increased my salary because business had improved so much. He seemed puzzled by the fact and did not connect it directly to my presence in the shop.

Glancing across at him now I recognized that it had not been a one-way thing. Since I had come here to work, my knowledge of books, particularly old, out-of-print editions, had increased tenfold and I had learned to respect Tom Ensley's great store of knowledge and expertise. I had even come to

51

appreciate the dour humour which had flurried me somewhat when I first worked for him. I had come to the conclusion that the somewhat austere façade was — just that — a façade. 'Mr Ensley,' I ventured somewhat hesitantly, 'how long have you known my aunt?'

Putting his finger carefully on the place where he was reading and looking at me over his spectacles he replied, 'A long time.' Not quite the answer I wanted, but it would have to suffice.

'Then you must know whether or not she was ever married?'

He looked startled by the question and hesitated for a moment before replying. 'Not as far as I recall.' His tone was cool but I persisted.

'But if you have known her all her life . . . ?' He hadn't actually said that; it was an assumption on my part.

'I have known her a long time but I have certainly not known her *all* of my life.'

I was puzzled — this was splitting hairs — what exactly did he mean?

'I lost track of her for several years when she lived in Australia. But to answer your question: as far as I know Grace never married.'

Well, that, I thought answered the question

I had not asked. She had not, could not, have a stepson.

'Australia? I never knew she had been there; she never mentioned it to me.'

'Probably not.' His tone was dry. 'I do not think it was one of the better periods of her life, which is probably why.' He glanced up at the old-fashioned station-type clock on the wall. 'If you are going for your lunch and to check on that dog maybe you should go.'

'Yes — yes I will.'

'Angela.' I turned back from the door.

'I won't be long,' I reassured him.

He dismissed that with a vague gesture. 'Oh take as long as you need. I was just going to suggest that it is high time we dropped the formality between us. I should like you to call me Tom in future.'

'Yes, of course Mr Ensley, if that is what you wish.'

'I do wish. Remember — Tom in future. It seems — well, more appropriate, now that we are the only two left.'

'Yes Mr — er — Tom.' I mumbled, getting the short Christian name past my lips with difficulty. It was only when I was hurrying along the street that I wondered what exactly he had meant when he said we were the only two left. I supposed he meant the only two who had really cared about Grace. But was that strictly true? My aunt had a great many friends and, of course, there was Billy. It was much later that I realized I had not actually asked about Grace's supposed stepson.

Billy bounded cheerfully out into the small patio garden when I opened the door. I felt a throb of pleasure that he was pleased to see me; then, aware that I was hungry, I reached for the loaf of bread and quickly made myself a cheese and tomato sandwich. I took it outside with a drink of apple juice and sat down on the one and only rustic chair that the tiny garden boasted. As I bit into my sandwich I noticed that the red ball had returned, but Billy was too interested in my sandwich to bother with it. When I had finished and given him a piece of cheese and some of the crust from my bread I got up and threw it for him. I played with him for a few minutes before a glance at my watch told me it was time to go back to work and I threw it back over the fence.

There was no opportunity to talk to Tom until we had a lull in the middle of the afternoon and he suggested a cup of tea.

'Did you mean that you and I were the only ones left who really knew Grace?' I asked. I had been about to say loved, but there was always something about Tom that stopped one from being in any way sentimental.

He stirred his tea thoughtfully. 'I suppose you could put it that way. I was thinking more of — well, of family.'

'Family, but . . . ' Somehow it seemed rude rather than blunt to say the words in my mind *But you weren't family*, and while I was searching in my head for an alternative the buzzer on the door announced another customer. I put down my half-finished mug of tea and hurried back to the front of the shop. The rest of the afternoon was busy and by closing time all I could think about was home.

The very first thing I saw was that damned red ball sitting on my tiny pocket handkerchief of grass once more. My first impulse was to charge outside and hurl it back; my second was to let Billy out to play with it; my third and the one I decided to follow was to ignore it and take the little dog for a walk instead. I knew that Grace walked him every day if she possibly could and, bearing that in mind, I had prudently brought his lead along with me. As soon as I clipped it on to his collar I remembered that I had no dog food. I decided to walk past the corner shop. There I would be able to buy a packet of dog biscuits and some tins of dog meat to last until I organized myself sufficiently to get some of the good fresh meat that I knew Grace fed him. Billy evinced such obvious pleasure when he saw his leash dangling from my hand that I decided to take the long way round to the local store, not the short cut across the park. But two tins of dog food and a packet of bone-shaped dog biscuits, plus bread and milk for myself were surprisingly heavy so I changed my mind and chose the shorter way home through the park instead.

I didn't see him disappear, just suddenly realized he was nowhere in sight.

'Billy!' Anxiety gave my voice an eldritch screech as, looking all around me, I frantically called his name. I bitterly regretted my inability to whistle as I knew that was how Grace called him back when he ran too far ahead of her, but it was a skill I had never been able to master. There must, I supposed, be something wrong with the shape of my lips or my teeth. I had once quoted the old saying: *A whistling woman and a crowing hen are good for neither God nor men* to Grace in self-defence when she had tried to teach me to whistle. I remembered her dry response, 'Well, I may not be much good for God, but I've never had any problem with men.' I remembered it because it had never quite fitted in with my inner view of my aunt.

Vowing to buy a proper dog whistle I opened my mouth and called again, as loudly as I could: 'B - i - l - l - y!' I closed my mouth hastily in some embarrassment as I realized that the few people walking in the park at this time of day were looking at me. I was almost — but not quite — prepared to give up and go home without him when I caught sight of a white rump and a perpendicular tail sticking out from a clump of bushes.

Swamped with both relief and annoyance I called sharply, 'Billy, come here!' He either didn't hear, or didn't want to, for the only response I got was the sight of the rear end of the little dog disappearing even further under the overhanging branches of the bush. Then, to my relief, I saw he was backing out. But he had something in his mouth. Though I was anxious to click the leash to his collar before he disappeared again, I stopped short in my tracks, heart thumping as I recognized the object Billy held triumphantly between his teeth. Head high and tail wagging he brought it to me. For a terrible moment I felt as if my breathing had stopped; then, with a sharp intake of breath I bent and retrieved Grace's silk scarf. It was the one she had worn when we had dinner together.

5

It was a very distinctive scarf; the background was a soft muted silver-grey-and-black pattern and superimposed over it were scattered bright pink roses. It was pure silk and expensive, as I knew — I had bought it myself from an exclusive boutique the previous Christmas. It was definitely not the sort of thing to be found in a chain store so the chance of it belonging to someone else was minimal. As I stared at it in the dog's mouth I remembered buying it and Grace's pleasure at receiving it. Always well-dressed and elegant, my aunt's taste was impeccable, if sometimes rather severe, and I did not always find it easy to choose a gift for her, so I had been especially pleased at the obvious pleasure with which the scarf was received and worn afterwards. I sometimes wondered how Grace managed to live the lifestyle she did and always look so elegant and well-dressed, but I assumed that she either had private means, or that her small antiques shop, which the unkind might well call a second-hand shop or even a junk shop, yielded a better income than appearances suggested.

I stood quite still, holding the scarf in my

hand, willing it to give up its secrets. Billy, gazing up at me, head on one side, was willing me to hand it back to him. After all it was his treasure — it smelled so deliciously of his beloved mistress — and he had found it. Neither of us had our wish granted.

Common sense told me that I should hand it in to the police at once. It was, I was sure, a vital piece of evidence, but, just like Billy, I longed to hang on to this precious and tangible reminder of my aunt. The last time I had seen the scarf it had been draped round Grace's shoulders in her inimitable way: apparently so casual and careless, yet I was sure my aunt had arranged it just as she wanted it. One of the reasons she always looked so elegant was that her appearance never seemed contrived. To take it to the police station meant turning round and retracing my steps so I stuffed it into my pocket and headed home.

Back inside my flat I pulled it out and held it up to my face. I imagined I could catch a whiff of Grace's perfume even though it had lain exposed to the night air. The faint scent reminded me of the enormity of the events of the last twenty-four hours. Overwhelmed by my loss I was suffused in a wave of emotion and, burying my face in the soft silk material, I let the tears fall. Even in my pain I knew I must surrender the scarf and explain how I had found it, but before I came to a decision the sudden shrill of the phone fractured the silence and penetrated my consciousness. I took a deep breath and leaned over the counter to snatch it up.

'Oh, Malcolm — hello.' In the stress of my discovery I had almost forgotten his existence.

'I just called to check up on you — make sure you are all right.'

'Yes, I — I'm fine, thank you.' While acknowledging to myself that it was kind of him to call me I did not like the idea of him, or anyone else, checking up on me.

'Are you sure? You don't sound it to me. Has anything happened?'

'Of course I'm sure I am all right,' I snapped. 'And what do you mean? Surely enough has happened in the last twenty-four hours to last for a while? What else were you expecting — my arrest or something?' Even to my own ears I sounded fraught — to say the least of it.

'Don't get emotional.' What the hell else did he expect me to be under the circumstances? 'I just meant . . . well, I thought you sounded as if you were crying when you picked up the phone.'

'And what if I was? I have every right

— and reason — to be upset. She was my aunt, my only living relation, and now this . . . ' My voice trailed away — I hadn't intended to mention the scarf. 'Why should anything happen? As far as I am concerned more than enough happened yesterday.' I did not find it soothing that I knew I was being unreasonable and that Malcolm was trying to be kind.

His sigh on the other end of the line was clearly audible, making me feel even worse. 'I meant . . . ' — he spoke with the slow patience one uses to a child who is being unreasonable — 'I just wondered if you had heard anything more from the police.'

'No, I haven't. As for me being upset, what do you expect, Malcolm? She was my aunt, my only relative, for goodness' sake. Why shouldn't I be upset?' I stopped short, aware that I was repeating myself.

'Yes — yes, of course. I know that, but to me you sounded as if something else had happened to upset you. Why did you say just then, *and now this*?'

'Like being accused of her murder do you mean?'

'There is no need to be facetious, darling.' The endearment was so unlike him that I imagined the word coming out through gritted teeth, but it succeeded in igniting a

61

spark of guilt within me, so I told him.

'I found, or rather Billy found, Grace's scarf.'

I thought Malcolm seemed irritated. Probably because I had mentioned Billy.

'What do you mean he found Grace's scarf? Where? In her flat again?'

'No. The police don't want people poking round at the moment. What I meant was exactly what I said. I was walking Billy back through the park — we had been to do some shopping and I took the short cut back because my basket was getting heavy . . . ' Malcolm sighed and I guessed he wanted me to get to the point. 'Well, like I said, we were walking through the park and Billy disappeared. I couldn't see him anywhere; I called his name and he came out from under a bush with something in his mouth. When I got close enough to see what it was I recognized Grace's scarf, the one she was wearing when she took me out to dinner. Are you still there?' I asked when the silence on the line lengthened.

'I'm still here. Are you quite sure it was Grace's scarf? After all, there are scarves everywhere — the shops are full of them — lots of women wear scarves.'

'I'm quite sure, Malcolm, it is one I gave her and I would recognize it anywhere.'

'What have you done about it? Did you take it to the police?'

'Not yet.'

I was surprised when after a few moments Malcolm said, 'Well, I don't suppose it is important; she probably lost it weeks ago. Threw it away or something.'

I started to protest that I knew that was wrong — Grace had been wearing the scarf when I had dinner with her. Then I remembered I had already mentioned that. Who was trying to convince whom of what?

'You are probably right,' I said with deliberate lightness and made up my mind to telephone the police as soon as I finished my conversation with Malcolm.

'I'll come round,' he told me 'You sound us if you need some cheering up.' How crass, I thought, as if he, or anyone, could cheer me up over the loss of Grace.

'No, don't bother. I'm just tired; I am going to have an early night. It was kind of you to call me.' But I was not all right, Malcolm's reaction when I told him about the scarf had been all wrong. I was frowning as I finished the conversation as quickly as I could. What possible reason could Malcolm have to disbelieve me about the scarf? Still frowning slightly I dialled the police station.

My word, that's quick I thought when my

doorbell rang a few minutes later. But when I opened the door it was my new neighbour, not the police, standing on the doorstep.

'If you want Jimmy's ball I threw it back,' was my immediate response, before I remembered that I hadn't done any such thing. I had thought about doing it, even meant to, then I'd decided to take Billy for a walk and do my shopping instead. 'No — sorry — I didn't, I meant to — but I — well — I didn't,' I finished lamely. 'I'll go and get it and give it to you.' I turned away from the door, intending to leave him where he was and hand the wretched ball over to him to take away. To my surprise and annoyance he stepped right inside after me.

'I'm here in response to your phone call,' he explained.

'Phone call?' I was nonplussed. 'But I didn't ring you.'

'You rang the police station.'

'Ye — e-s — but . . . '

'I am working on the case.'

'The case?' I hadn't yet thought of Grace's death as a case.

'I understand you have found — '

The doorbell ringing again interrupted him. This time it was a uniformed policeman who confronted me.

'Miss Divine? Angela Divine?' I wasn't

quite sure whether he was asking me or telling me who I was by the tone of his voice, but I was sure that this was a genuine policeman. So what was the man who had just walked calmly into my house playing at?

I gathered my wits enough to admit I was Angela Divine. 'Please come in,' I almost begged, pulling the door open. The policeman followed me inside. To my surprise when he saw my visitor he just nodded; almost as if he had expected to find him in my flat. 'How did you get here before me?' His voice had a friendly ring.

'I was in the police station when Angela rang to say she had found the scarf. I came to see what she could tell me.'

'You press people have noses like bloodhounds and skins like leather,' the police officer told him. 'You shouldn't have let him in,' he added to me.

'But I thought he was you!' I protested, before realizing that he was not serious. I didn't like anyone, certainly not the police, thinking I was completely stupid and naïve.

'Did he claim to be a police officer?'

'Well . . . ' I began, before the person I still thought of as my next-door neighbour interrupted.

'I merely said I was working on the case; perfectly true, but I omitted to tell you that I am an investigative journalist, who would like to be a private eye. My name is Derek by the way.' The smile he bestowed on me was so full of sympathy, warmth and — yes, a hint of humour, that I could not help but smile back. Annoyed with myself I managed to change my expression to one of exasperation.

'You meant me to think you were something to do with the police,' I told him, and promptly wished I hadn't. Before my mouth said anything else I didn't want it to I addressed my next words directly to the police officer. 'I was walking through the park with Billy . . . '

'Billy?' he queried.

'My dog — well, actually he was my aunt's dog. I brought him back here with me after — after the discovery of — of my aunt's body.' I stumbled over the words, then continued to explain how Billy had run off and disappeared under the bushes, to reappear with Grace's scarf in his mouth.

'I see. If he was Grace Arbuthnot's dog that would explain why he found the scarf and dragged it out of its hiding-place.' He seemed to be lost in his own thoughts for a moment; then said, 'You are quite sure it was hers?' Briefly I wondered if Malcolm had put his theory forward about the scarf.

'Absolutely sure. I gave it to her myself for

Christmas. It — it was quite exclusive and expensive so I do not think there would be many identical ones about. I had dinner with her the night she was murdered.' The young officer nodded a tad impatiently; I was just repeating what he already knew. My voice cracked as I added, 'She was wearing it then.'

'You are sure about that?'

'Of course I am.' I was getting tired of every word I said doubted, or so it seemed. I turned on my neighbour who had pulled out a notepad and was hurriedly jotting notes in what appeared to be shorthand. 'Do you have to do that?'

The police officer turned at my words. 'It would be greatly appreciated if you could be very careful what you write at this stage. Too much information could alert the guilty person that we are on to him, or her, it could also put Miss Divine in danger.'

I blinked; until now it hadn't occurred to me that I myself might actually be in danger.

'You do realize, of course,' the police officer continued, 'that you are the last person to have seen Grace Arbuthnot alive?'

I swallowed and nodded. 'Does that make me the prime suspect?' I croaked.

The officer looked at me for a moment, then smiled, as if the idea was absurd. Even though I knew perfectly well that I was entirely innocent I felt a wash of relief. 'Not necessarily. But you could certainly be in danger if the killer thinks you are in possession of evidence or knowledge that might incriminate him — or her.' He pulled out a card and passed it to me. 'You can ask for me at the police station — I am assigned to this case. If you think of anything else, or you hear or see something, however trivial, that might have any connection, however slight, with your aunt's death, get in touch with me. In the meantime I will take this with me.' He picked up the scarf from where it lay on the counter top between us. 'Don't forget if anything, anything at all, rings alarm bells get in touch immediately. If I am not available then speak to somebody else.'

I gulped and nodded. Until now my strongest emotion had been grief for my aunt, now it was laced with fear for myself. 'Yes, I will,' I promised.

He turned at the door. 'One other thing — don't talk about this to too many people,' he advised.

I expected my other visitor to follow him out, but he was still standing there, leaning nonchalantly against the counter top and running his eye down the notes he had made when I turned back into the room. I wished I could read them. I also hoped he did not

68

intend publishing too much of whatever he had written. I watched him flip the notebook closed and put it, together with his Biro, in the breast pocket of his jacket.

'I had better get your ball,' I offered, in a voice that was far from steady.

'Not to worry — I've already thrown it back over the fence.'

'You mean . . . ' I began, but let the words fade away. Maybe it wasn't too diplomatic to accuse him of coming into my property when I was out or unaware of his presence there. All the same, I didn't like the idea at all.

'When I came to the door just now.' Irritatingly he had read my thoughts accurately. 'Well, I'll be off if you don't need me any more.' Before I could retort tartly that I had never needed him he added, 'Don't worry — I don't intend to write anything at all at the moment.' He patted the pocket where he had put the notebook and looked directly into my eyes. 'Don't forget — like the copper I am only a phone call away. Or you can yell over the fence.' His smile warmed me but he left me confused and not a little anxious, when he left with a brief 'Good-night.'

6

I had never been afraid of living alone before. On the contrary I had always revelled in my freedom and independence; now I would have given anything for company, preferably large, strong, reliable male company. Chiding myself for my weakness I reached for the dog food, rummaged in the drawer for my can opener and set about feeding Billy, reminding myself that I was not entirely alone. But, as I put the bowl of food down on the floor in front of the little dog, I realized this was scant comfort, he hadn't been able to save Grace.

As the light faded I pulled the curtains across all the windows, having made sure that each one was closed and snibbed. Then I checked and double-checked that the door was locked and the safety chain in place. I put a CD in the player to cheer myself up, then turned it off; wouldn't it be better to hear someone trying to get in than to be taken by surprise?

By this time I was in too much of a dither to think about getting a decent meal and settled for beans on toast topped by a poached egg. After that I decided to go to bed. I encouraged Billy to jump on my bed; it was encouragement he didn't need at all as he had already decided that that was definitely the most comfortable spot. Apart from the fact that he insisted on sleeping on my feet so that I couldn't stretch my legs out his presence certainly gave me some comfort. Convinced I would not sleep a wink I tried to work out the scenario that had led to Grace's scarf being found in the park. It was not a comforting line of thought, as all ideas — however bizarre — inevitably ended up with the unpalatable truth that Grace had been murdered. I tried the opposite tack — not thinking about it at all. Not thinking about something, I discovered, was even more difficult than thinking about it so I just let my thoughts drift wherever they would.

*   *   *

The next time I thought about what to think the early morning sun was creeping between the curtains at my bedroom window and a glance at my alarm clock told me its imperative summons would rouse me in exactly three minutes' time. I reached out and depressed the button, then got out of bed before I had a chance to drop off to sleep again. To my surprise and considerable relief I felt wide awake and reasonably confident that I could face the day ahead, and whatever it brought. With this bracing thought I strode to the shower. My confidence stayed with me until, clean and refreshed, I pulled back the curtains at my window, then it dissipated to become irritation at the sight of a large red ball right in the middle of my pocket-handkerchief patch of grass. I didn't waste time asking myself how it had got there. It was all too obvious; it had been thrown over by that wretched man next door, or the equally tiresome child. It was time to put a stop to this. It was verging on harassment.

Bristling with righteous indignation I marched outside, grabbed the ball and chucked it back.

After the somewhat unnerving experience the previous evening when I walked Billy in the park I decided to take him to the bookshop with me. It was a pleasant little walk of about twenty minutes, enough with the walk home at the end of the day to give both Billy and me sufficient exercise. There was plenty of room at the back of the shop, where there was not only a small kitchen but also a backyard that was actually larger than my own outside area. Tom and Grace had been friends, so I did not think he would object.

My first impulse was to turn back into the room and answer the phone, which rang just as I reached the door. Almost certainly it was only my neighbour demanding the return of his cursed ball. I hesitated for a nanosecond before I pulled the door shut. I refused to entertain the thought that it might be someone else and set out briskly on the walk to work with Billy trotting along happily at my side.

'Ah!' Tom Ensley stared at me over the top of his hornrimmed spectacles. It was a habit he had and one that seemed suitably to impress people with his intelligence and learning. 'I see you have Grace's little dog. I meant to suggest to you yesterday that you might bring him to work with you. Are you coping with him?'

I looked at him in surprise; I thought it an odd question. 'Fine — just fine. To tell you the truth I am glad of his company. Grace was so attached to him — she would probably have haunted me if I had let the police take him.' I broke off with an apologetic half-laugh, realizing that my feeble attempt at levity had not been well received. Tom's expression as he looked at me suggested he thought my remark in very bad taste. I began to mumble an apology but he cut me short.

'Probably,' he agreed absently, his expression and tone of voice making me wonder if he had even heard my facetious remark. 'Quite so, I'm glad you have dealt with him; I can't say I'd have wanted to take him on. I always thought Grace spoilt him.'

I bridled at this slur on both Billy and Grace. I ignored this remark and pressed on. 'So you don't mind if I bring him here? I didn't like to leave him at home — not after last night.'

'What happened last night?' His tone was sharp and I noted that I now had his full attention. After a moment's hesitation I explained briefly how Billy had found Grace's scarf. 'I thought — well, I thought someone — you know — whoever — well, someone might bear a grudge against Billy; they might wonder what he would find next so I didn't like the idea of leaving him alone.' This explanation sounded halting and confused even to myself, but I still found it incredibly hard actually to put into words what had happened to my aunt.

'Quite right — quite right . . . ' Tom agreed. 'I would have done the same myself; bad enough the poor little beggar being orphaned as it were, don't like to think he could be on someone's hit list, even if he isn't quite my favourite person.' He smiled at me to show he had no ill feelings towards the dog. 'Better pop him in the back now,' he added, as the first customer of the day appeared outside the glass door. He crossed to the door to turn the sign to OPEN and let them in, leaving me to dispose of Billy at the rear of the shop. I heard the phone ring as I went. When I came back into the shop Tom turned towards me holding out the receiver. He put his hand over the mouthpiece and his lips formed the words: 'Grace's lawyers.'

I wanted to ask what they wanted, but Tom was shaking the phone impatiently as he held it towards me and turned to a customer who was approaching him with a couple of books in hand and an expression that suggested he wanted to ask something.

'Have I Miss Angela Divine on the line?' an efficient female voice asked as I put the receiver to my ear.

'You have.' I found myself answering in the same vein.

'We would like you to come round to our office as soon as convenient,' the voice continued. 'Please ask to see our Mr Smethurst and please bring something with which to identify yourself.'

'Yes — ma'am!' I was tempted to reply, but merely asked, 'Do I need to make an appointment?'

'No . . . ' I could hear mumbled voices in the background, then, 'Well, yes — it might be better if you did. Mr Smethurst is very busy and he particularly wants to see you himself.'

'I . . . see,' I murmured, feeling a strange reluctance to obey this summons. 'May I ring you back?' I grabbed a Biro and hastily scribbled down the number I was given on the pad that Tom always kept on the desk.

'But of course you must go. If it is something to do with Grace it could be important,' was Tom's immediate reaction when I relayed the content of the phone call to him. 'See if you can go in your lunch hour.'

When I arrived at the offices of Smethurst, Smethurst & Smethurst I was told at the reception desk to make my way upstairs and I would see Mr Smethurst's office directly opposite the top of the flight.

I followed the instructions, wondering, as I made my way up what seemed a very long and very steep flight of steps with a bend halfway up, whether it was premature ageing or nerves that made me catch my breath when I reached the top. I paused and inhaled deeply, but before I could tap on the door in front of me it opened and a most personable young man smiled at me. As my preconceived notion of Mr Smethhurst had been an elderly, scholarly-looking man with wispy white hair, all in all a Dickensian figure, I assumed he was a client leaving the office and was surprised when he smiled warmly and stood back for me to walk in. A quick mental retake told me that that this must be the '& Smethurst' of the Smethurst, Smethurst & Smethurst as he closed the door behind me and followed me into his office. The room, I was relieved to find, was light, airy, and very modern, not in the least musty or Dickensian. True, the shelves were packed with files, and serious-looking reference books on law but the computer, printer, scanner and phone bank on the large desk were what dominated the room.

'Do sit down.' Josh Smethurst pointed to the chair on my side of the desk as he walked round to take the one opposite me. 'You are, I understand, Angela Divine and you are the niece of the late Grace Arbuthnot?' I nodded and fumbled in my bag.

'I have my driving licence here. I was told to bring something that would identify me.' I had intended to bring my birth certificate but couldn't find it. I supposed I must have had it at some time and no doubt when I stopped looking it would turn up. 'Is this enough?' I asked anxiously. I hoped he wouldn't say 'No' and put me down as an impostor. He smiled slightly and after a perfunctory glance at my licence waved it away. Josh Smethurst looked totally relaxed and anything but intimidating with his hands folded on the desktop and his light-grey eyes on my face.

'No need for that,' he assured me. 'I know you are Angela Divine.' Feeling rather foolish I tucked my licence back in my wallet. He swivelled his chair round so that his back was to me and he was facing the large filing cabinet that stood against the wall behind the desk. From one of the drawers he drew out a large manila envelope and handed it to me. To my surprise I saw it had my own name in large letters on the front. He placed it on the desk between us and tapped it with the forefinger of his right hand as if to emphasize what he had to tell me.

'Your aunt deposited this with us some years ago,' he told me. 'From time to time, approximately once a year, she retrieved it, took it home and returned it a few days later for safe keeping. I don't know why; I can only guess that either she needed to check that the contents were still there or to update them in some manner. My father's instructions were to keep it safe and hand it over to you as soon as possible after her death, and to you only. Should you predecease her' — he gave me a deprecating little smile as he said this — 'the envelope was to be destroyed. On no account was it to be handed to anyone other than you.

Since my father retired I have dealt with your aunt's affairs including her will.'

I nodded. It didn't seem necessary to point out that I knew nothing whatsoever about Smethurst, Smethurst & Smethurst, not even that they were Grace's solicitors. I would dearly have liked to ask if he knew whether or not Grace really had a stepson. I think it was because in my heart I didn't believe he existed that I kept silent. I reached across the desk to pick up the large package which the lawyer was now pushing towards me. I thought he looked as if he would be very glad to get rid of it and wondered what it could contain.

As I picked it up he got to his feet in an obvious gesture of dismissal, making me feel that the envelope was not the only thing he was anxious to see leave his office.

'Thank you for coming.' He smiled as he shook my hand. 'I expect I shall see more of you when we come to deal with Miss Arbuthnot's will.'

I murmured vague and polite farewells as I left his office. I had not thought about a will, but of course Grace would have left one. She was not the type of person who would fail to leave her affairs in order.

7

I got back to the shop with some of my lunch break still to spare. There I found a couple of customers peacefully browsing and Tom sharing a cheese sandwich with Billy. I raised my eyebrows. 'Has Billy been promoted to shop assistant?' I asked with a smile.

'Oh, higher than that,' Tom assured me. 'He is assistant manager now.' He rubbed his palms together and held his hands out to the little dog in a gesture intended to show that the sandwich was finished. Billy immediately turned his attention to me and with gyrating body and wagging tail greeted me warmly back to the fold.

'Shut him in the back.' Tom seemed to regret his moment of weakness. 'Make us both a cup of coffee then tell me what you learned from Messrs Smethurst, Smethurst & Smethurst.'

I shrugged deprecatingly. 'Not much at the moment,' I told him. 'I was just handed this envelope and dismissed.'

Tom eyed the bulky package with obvious curiosity but he said nothing. I, filled with an odd reluctance to discover its contents, afraid

I might find myself in possession of some knowledge I would really rather live without, took it with me into the back room where I laid it to one side with my handbag. I busied myself making coffee and another cheese sandwich which, of course, Billy expected to share.

I ate my snack lunch quickly, debating whether to open the envelope now or take it home with me at the end of the day and wait till I was alone. Not that I really minded Tom knowing what it contained; I supposed it was some cussedness in my own personality that made me resist satisfying his curiosity. In the end the decision was taken out of my own hands; as I was turning the OPEN sign on the door to CLOSED at the end of an unusually busy afternoon Tom suggested a quick cuppa to round the day off. I could open my envelope while we drank it.

'You make a pot of tea while I cash up,' he said. Satisfying his curiosity seemed the easiest option.

He was like a small boy who couldn't wait to get into his Christmas stocking, I mused sentimentally, as he leaned forward slightly across the table while I slid my thumb under the flap of the envelope. 'It doesn't look very exciting to me,' I murmured, drawing out a clear plastic document bag filled with what appeared to be typewritten pages. I stared at them in bewilderment; there must be at least 200 sheets. On top of the pile was a folded piece of paper.

I removed it and, as I unfolded it, Tom, who was still looking at the pile of paper, remarked, 'It looks like the manuscript of a book.'

'I think that is what it is,' I agreed, as I read quickly through the single sheet of paper, which I recognized as a letter from Grace to myself.

'Good God!' he exploded. 'It's just the typescript of one of her bloody books!'

A quick perusal of the pile of papers proved that it was indeed the manuscript of a book, but what did Tom mean by his outburst?

'What do you mean?' I wanted to know as I gave the letter in my hand my full attention. 'She explains it, more or less, here. She says it is the manuscript of her unfinished book. What does she mean?'

'Are you telling me you didn't know?' he asked. 'Well, all I can say is she was a very dark horse, your aunt.'

I thought I was beginning to understand; this was a book my aunt had written, or had been in the process of writing. Tom had talked about her books in the plural. Did that mean she had written more? I turned back to the single sheet in my hand and frowned, trying to take in exactly what was written there. I read it out loud, hoping that actually hearing the words would clarify them. 'Does this mean that she was someone else beside Grace Arbuthnot — someone called Faith Treloar? That's the name on this pile of papers. She says she is giving me Faith Treloar. What does she mean?'

'That's one of the fancy names she wrote her books under; it would seem she expected you to take it on. It's not another person.' Tom sounded irritated by my stupidity. 'She is giving you the name and copyright in her books,' he explained. 'Have you ever read any?'

'Aunt Grace's books, do you mean, or this Treloar woman?' I still hadn't worked my head around the fact that they were actually one and the same person.

'Well, this Treloar woman — as you call her — is Grace. You work in a bookshop so you must know that lots of writers use a pen-name rather than their own. We may even have some of her books; I can't say I have read any myself, not quite my preferred reading, but you might have read some.'

It was my turn to be irritated now by the implied slur on both Grace's and my own intellectual qualities. I shook my head; I couldn't remember reading any. Yet there was a vague familiarity about the name. 'I think I have seen a couple of her books on the shelves.'

'They will be in the romantic fiction section if you have,' Tom told me as he headed back into the shop. I felt Grace and her scribblings had been dismissed, but I went to the fiction shelves to look for her books. My curiosity had been piqued to discover this hitherto unknown aspect of Grace.

I found two and pulled them off the shelves. They were in the romantic fiction section but when I read the blurbs and flicked through the pages I decided they were definitely a step up from the girl-meets-boy type of book. I saw that both had been published a few years ago. I looked up and saw that Tom was watching me.

'You can take those home and read them if you want to,' he told me magnanimously. 'You'd have to go to a new-book shop to see any later ones.'

'Or the library,' I pointed out. I looked down at my watch. It didn't close for another half-hour but it was out of my way. I decided it would be quicker and easier and I would probably learn more if I looked up Faith Treloar and her books on the Internet.

I couldn't wait to get home and fire up my computer. How many more surprises in Grace's life would surface, I wondered? First an unknown stepson, whom I still refused to believe existed, and now the discovery that there was a different persona hidden behind the façade I had always known. I reflected sadly that however many surprises I turned up or that presented themselves to me nothing could have a more shocking impact than Grace's sudden death. Eager to get indoors and start my cyber-sleuthing I was anything but pleased to find my next-door neighbour on my doorstep.

'Did you want something?' Even as I listened to my own chilly tones I thought: what a stupid thing to say — of course he wanted something or he wouldn't be standing there. Only my natural politeness had prevented a curt *What do you want?*

'If you are after your little boy's ball, I threw it back,' I told him, as I fumbled in my bag for the key. Billy was wagging his tail ingratiatingly and looking up into the young man's face. I was irritated to the point of annoyance with him. Billy should have warned me he was there: growled or something; instead he was obviously pleased to see him.

'No, I am not after the ball, and Jimmy is not my little boy.'

'Oh, but I thought you said . . . ' I floundered, feeling as if somehow I had been wrong-footed. 'When I saw you looking for the ball — the day you moved in . . . ' My voice petered out as I realized he was watching me with a slightly sardonic smile.

'I said the ball belonged to Jimmy and that I had just moved in. I am afraid you put two and two together and made five.' He was looking at me strangely and I remembered this was a re-run of a conversation we had already had.

'Yes, yes of course, he is your nephew,' I remembered, feeling, and sure I looked, very foolish. He went on to repeat the information anyway.

'Jimmy is my nephew — my sister's little boy — I was looking after him temporarily while she was moving house. Now let me introduce myself properly. As neighbours we should at least try to be on good terms, don't you think?' There was a facetious note in his voice that made me colour up. He held out his hand to me, 'Derek — Derek Royle.'

I reluctantly took the proffered hand but before I could say anything he added, 'You are Angela Divine, Grace Arbuthnot's niece.'

'We both know that,' I snapped. Was my relationship to a murder victim always going to be the defining point about me? His grip tightened on my hand. I was left standing there feeling, if possible, more foolish than ever. 'Yes,' I snapped. 'Not a very clever deduction as you already knew that. Now, can I have my hand back please?'

'You can — on condition you give me five minutes of your time. I need to talk to you.'

I looked round but there was no one in sight and I could not think of a good excuse off the top of my head not to talk to him. Besides, Billy was still wagging his tail vigorously. Perhaps I could trust his judgement. 'All right,' I said grudgingly. 'You had better come in. I don't particularly want to stand out here.' I bit off the words: *where everyone can see us.*

His smile, which I had already registered as rather nice, said the words for me, adding ' . . . holding hands.'

I snatched my hand free, bestowed on him what I firmly hoped was a withering look and fumbled for my key.

As we stepped inside Billy's whole demeanour changed. The friendly little dog who had greeted Derek disappeared; a low growl rumbled up from him followed by a shrill yelp of a bark that made me jump and drop my keys as I fumbled for the light in the rather dim hallway. Immediately I saw the totally chaotic mess that my small, but normally very neat, home had become. I let out a yelp of horror very similar to the noise Billy had just made, and for the same reason: shock and a need to boost my swiftly flagging nerves, before my hand went up to my face and covered my mouth.

'Oh — my God!' I gasped, breathless with horror. I turned beseeching eyes on my companion as if he might know who the perpetrator was, or at least the reason for this vandalism. 'What — who — why?' I demanded, my eyes filling with tears of rage; then, as another thought hit me, 'How did they get in?'

Before either of my questions was answered there was a thud, recognizable as feet landing on firm lawn, then the sound of running footsteps. We turned back as one to the still open door and were just in time to see a figure disappearing at high speed in the gathering dusk. Derek ran outside but turned back in seconds, looking crestfallen. 'Too late — there was a car waiting; I didn't even manage to get the number. Sorry.'

'Not your fault,' I muttered, moving further into the tiny unit to inspect the damage. Furniture was overturned, drawers emptied, their contents tipped out on the floor, cupboard doors had been left open. I looked at the disarray and felt sick. This was my home and it had been violated. Feeling a sudden draught I walked into the tiny bathroom. The sash window was open, a bottle of shampoo had been knocked off the shelf above the washbasin and the slippery liquid was spilled on the floor with pieces of broken glass sticking up from it like small islands. I saw it too late and slipped, hitting my head on the side of the bath as I went down.

When I opened my eyes I was on the little couch in my lounge. I felt disorientated and rubbed my head ruefully where a large bump was already appearing.

'What happened?' I asked, frowning in confusion at the chaos around me, the presence of my next-door neighbour and the heavy perfume.

'You had an unwelcome visitor who left a bit of mess, then you slipped on the shampoo all over the floor.'

I sniffed. 'Is that what I can smell?' I asked. 'But why on earth was shampoo on the floor in the first place?'

'Knocked off the shelf by whoever-it-was when he made his getaway. Stay where you are,' he added, when I made a halfhearted attempt to get up. 'You were lucky you didn't cut yourself on the broken glass, but your luck might not hold, so just stay there while I clear up the mess.'

I watched through the open door as he carefully brushed up two pieces of glass from the pool of slippery, scented liquid on the floor. He took the dustpan into the tiny kitchen and emptied it into the waste bin. 'What shall I use to mop it up?' he asked, looking round to see if anything suggested itself.

'Oh, use the towels in the bathroom,' I told him, dropping back on to the sofa as he made *stay there* gestures with his hand. 'Then pop them in the washing machine, at least I won't need to put in any soap powder when I wash them!'

Derek mopped up the mess, then obediently put the soaked towels into the drum of the small washing-machine. I hoped they wouldn't create so many suds when I turned the machine on that I had another mess to clear up.

'Now,' he told me, 'I am going to make a cup of tea while we wait for the police, then I will help you straighten up.' He peered at me anxiously. 'What about that bump? Shouldn't you have something on it?'

I shook my head, then, when the action proved more painful than I had expected I said, 'I'll soak a wad of cotton wool in witch hazel, that will help.'

'Tell me where it is and I will get it for you. You can be holding it to your head while I make the tea.'

I held the cooling and soothing wad of damp cotton wool to the rapidly rising bump on my temple and watched him deftly making tea. I tried to get my thoughts round the cosy intimacy of the situation, in such stark contrast to the way I had felt about this man only a few short minutes ago.

I was aware that Derek watched me anxiously as I sipped the tea he passed me. 'I don't take that much sugar,' I told him, wrinkling my nose at the sweetness.

'Good for shock,' was his unperturbed response. 'Have you any idea, any idea at all, what whoever it was who did this was looking for?' he asked, sipping his own tea.

I shook my head and immediately regretted it. 'No idea at all. Anyone can see I haven't exactly got the place crammed with priceless antiques or valuables of any sort,' I told him.

Derek looked thoughtful, peering into his cup as if he might find the answer there. 'Any thoughts at all?'

'No — I haven't. Is there anything you might be able to tell me about the person you saw escaping?'

Derek shook his head. 'Afraid not. There was a car at the kerb, engine running. He hurled himself in and was gone.' He looked thoughtful for a moment. 'Did you see it when you got home? Was it there then?'

'No, at least I didn't notice it and surely I would have done if it had been parked anywhere near my door.'

'I should imagine so. It could have been waiting just out of sight up the road and moved when you went inside, guessing that whoever it was in there would come out very quickly. Unless they stayed to bash you up.' He added the last bit with a teasing grin in my direction.

I let that remark pass. 'So . . . there must have been two people involved,' I said thoughtfully. 'You don't think it was some kid breaking in for a bit of a lark?'

'I wish it were,' Derek said cryptically He frowned and his eyes took on a look of concentration, as if he were trying to remember something important that could help. 'I didn't have a chance to get a good look at the car, or get the number, but I rather think from the general shape of it that it was a BMW,' he said slowly.

'A BMW? Are you certain?'

'Well, no — I couldn't say I was absolutely certain. Just that I had a sort of impression that that was what it was. Do you know anyone who drives one?'

I stared at him. I did, but the thought that Malcolm could have anything to do with this was absurd. I pressed my lips together, but Derek's face suddenly took on an *Ah ha* expression and he snapped his fingers. 'I saw someone driving a BMW only this morning.' The excitement in his voice faded as he remembered. 'It was your boyfriend — Malcolm.'

'Well, there is no way he could have had anything to do with someone breaking in here. Why on earth should he? If there was something he wanted he only had to ask me . . . ' My voice trailed away; was I protesting too vehemently? No, of course not. There simply was no possible reason for Malcolm to have had anything to do with it. I looked at Derek and saw he was watching me keenly as if trying to gauge my expression or my feelings, and whether or not I meant what I was saying. Catching me looking at him he smiled quickly.

'When the police are done, I'll help you straighten up if you like — if you feel up to it?'

I didn't, but the offer of help was one I was unable to resist.

8

'I think that is about it.' My sigh was a mingling of relief, gratitude and sheer exhaustion as I looked round the lounge now restored, like the rest of the flat, to some semblance of order. I managed a shaky smile before collapsing into the nearest chair. 'Well, this room anyway — I don't know about me!' I rubbed the rising bump on my head ruefully.

'You are lucky it wasn't worse,' Derek remarked as he watched me.

'You're a real comfort,' I told him sourly, and then regretted it. After all, what he had said was absolutely true. I sighed and made a move as if to hoist myself up out of the chair.

'Stay put!' Derek held out his hand in a gesture that made me think of a policeman on point duty. 'I think this is another moment when the ubiquitous cup of tea is called for; unless, of course, you feel the need for something stronger?'

'Tea.' I realized that my response could hardly be called gracious. 'Please,' I added as a belated afterthought. 'If you put the kettle on I will make it.'

'Stay where you are.'

'This is becoming a habit.' My voice was grumpy but I managed a rather weak smile. I should have been grateful; instead I felt cranky, unable to be gracious in my weakness.

I closed my eyes and let myself be soothed by the sound of Derek looking after me.

'You don't really think Malcolm had something to do with this.' I asked Derek over the rim of my teacup. Derek looked thoughtful and did not return my rather wobbly smile. He closed both hands round his own cup and stared into its depths. He took a long slow drink before asking, 'Is there anyone else you can think of — anyone at all — who drives a BMW?'

I shook my head at first, then I too frowned. 'Well, yes, of course. Tom does. But it is even more absurd to think of him having anything to do with this business than to think Malcolm could be involved.'

'Who is Tom and why would it be so absurd?'

'Tom is my boss. He owns the bookshop where I work. I didn't think of him because I don't often see him in his car, and because — well, it is too ridiculous to think he could have had anything at all to do with it.'

'Why?'

I was startled into looking up at him when

he fired the single word at me. 'Well, it just is. He's my boss and he was also Grace's friend. Grace knew of my passion for books. I was surprised she didn't tell me he was looking for someone to work in his second-hand bookshop. I knew of the shop — who doesn't? — and jumped at the job when I saw the advert.'

'You enjoy working there?'

'I love it. What Tom doesn't know about books you could put on a postage stamp. I've learned so much since I have worked for him.'

'Don't you find it a bit dull — even lonely at times — just the two of you? I mean, you are a young and attractive woman and he is — well — older.'

'Not really. There are always people coming into the shop and, like I said, I've learned so much since I've been there. The second-hand book business is so different from selling new books. Apart from anything else there is always the possibility that something really rare and valuable might turn up one day in a nondescript box of old books. We have a rare books section and Tom goes to auctions sometimes looking for special editions or to try and find something one of his customers is looking for. But you know what the shop is like — you have been there.'

'I thought most of that sort of thing was done on the Internet these days?'

'Yes it is, I suppose. But Tom is not so computer literate as I am so I help him with that side of things too. But considering he is so immersed in the book business and knows so much about them it is odd he didn't appear to know much about Grace's books . . . ' I mused, then stopped abruptly, afraid to voice my thoughts.

'What are you talking about?' Derek looked puzzled.

'Oh . . . ' I shrugged. 'It turns out Grace wrote books in her free time. A sort of hobby I suppose — like some people knit.'

'And you didn't know about it?' He sounded surprised, disbelieving almost. My eyes travelled across the room to the package lying where I had put it what now seemed an aeon ago when I opened the door on the chaos in my home. Derek saw my shift of focus and his eyes followed mine. For some reason I wondered if I should have told him about Grace's *alter ego* as I waited for him to ask me about it. That bump on the head and the shock of finding my place turned over had made me paranoid, I thought; what harm could there possibly be in telling him how I had learned about Grace's novels, or even showing him the contents of the envelope?

But even as I was thinking this I heard a car draw up and footsteps sounded outside the door. 'Oh, my God! I had completely forgotten — I promised to go out with Malcolm for a drink.'

Derek stood up. 'In that case I won't keep you. But I'd lay off the hard stuff and stick to fruit juice if I were you after that bump on the head.'

I automatically put up my hand, fingered the lump and winced. 'You are probably right,' I conceded with a brief smile. 'Thanks a lot, Derek, for all you have done for me — ' I broke off as I heard Malcolm at the door.

He shrugged. 'I guess anyone would have done the same.' He spoke coolly and, dropping his voice to a whisper, asked, 'Is there another way out of here?'

'Bathroom window — remember?' I whispered back, finding it amusing the lengths Derek was prepared to go to avoid a face-to-face confrontation with Malcolm. As I opened the door I thought I heard Derek dropping lightly to the ground at the back of the flat.

'Gosh, sorry I'm not ready.' I gushed an apology and cursed myself for sounding like a breathless schoolgirl overcome with guilt. 'I'll be as quick as I can.' I hurried into the bathroom, checked the window was closed properly. I snibbed the catch across so that it couldn't be opened from the outside and pulled down the blind. I applied my make-up up more heavily than usual and pulled my hair as far forward as possible to cover up the bump and bruise on my temple. Then, after a critical look at myself in the mirror, I changed my shoes and flung a long coat with a faux-fur collar over my clothes.

'I'm ready . . . 'I began as I went back into the living room. I stopped on the threshold when I saw that Malcolm was searching through some magazines and papers on the table. My voice was cool even though the anger that coursed through my veins was white hot.

'What are you looking for?' I wanted to know, as I stepped forward to take the manuscript from him.

Malcolm's smile was urbane with only the barest hint of apology; he turned. 'Nothing at all — as you can see.' Although he replaced the papers on the table I felt that he was reluctant to do so, but he smiled as he turned to me. 'If you are ready, let's go.'

As I settled in the passenger seat I wished myself anywhere but where I was. My head was still aching with a dull throb; I felt tired, thoroughly confused and, yes, I was forced to admit it to myself, more than a little scared.

Why on earth hadn't I remembered earlier that I was going out with Malcolm? There would have been time then to ring him up with some good excuse or other, even maybe the truth, and cancel the date. I stole a sideways glance at him and wondered why I was suddenly wary of admitting to him what had happened. A few days ago I would have had no qualms in doing so.

He took me to a popular drinking-place; the sort, I thought cynically, where the upwardly mobile went to be seen as much as to drink. Thankfully the lighting was dim and without consulting Malcolm I headed for a table in a particularly poorly lit and secluded corner. It was the sort usually grabbed by couples who wanted to be in their own secluded world. Malcolm must have thought that that was my motive in choosing it, for he leaned over me. 'Your usual, darling?' he murmured, his voice intimate.

'I'll just have an orange juice, please.'

Raising one eyebrow he asked, 'Have you taken the pledge or something?'

'No, I just don't feel like alcohol tonight.' I didn't offer any explanation.

'You are quite sure?' he persisted before moving across to the bar with a slight shrug.

It was my fault that thereafter the evening was not a success. I simply could not make the effort to be entertaining.

'I can't say being on the wagon improves your conversation,' Malcolm remarked drily.

'I'm sorry — really I am, Malcolm. It's just that I feel so tired and my head aches.' Absently I pushed my hair back as I spoke and Malcolm leaned towards me; even in the dim light he had seen my bruise.

'What on earth have you done to yourself?'

'What do you mean?' I stammered, playing for time.

'That bruise — and a lump, isn't it? How did you get that?'

'Oh, that. I — er — I walked into a door.'

'Well, if you don't want to tell me at least think up a better excuse than that old chestnut.' He drained his glass and stood up. 'Come on — I'm taking you home.'

I followed him, feeling a mixture of relief and guilt. I really had nothing at all on which to base the most slender suspicion of him but some inner gut feeling insisted that if he himself hadn't broken into my flat he knew who had. I was enormously relieved to be on my way home to my bed.

'I won't ask you in — I'm not very good company tonight,' I apologized when we reached my front door.

'I don't need an invitation, I'm coming in. Someone has to see that you get to bed and try and sleep that off,' he told me firmly as he waited for me to unlock the door. 'Now, you get into bed and I will make you a hot drink. Tea, chocolate — what would you like?'

'Chocolate, I think.' I bit off the words *I've had enough tea* and mumbled my thanks.

He shooed me away from my cupboards in the tiny kitchen. 'I can find things. You just get into bed. Have you any aspirin, Panadol, anything?'

I nodded. 'In the bathroom.'

A short time later I was sitting up in bed smiling at Malcolm over a large mug of hot milky chocolate and nibbling at the biscuits he had insisted I ate. He really was being extraordinarily kind, I thought drowsily, feeling so relaxed I wondered if the Panadol were already taking effect. He watched me eat and drink, then he removed the tray. Seconds later I heard him rinsing the plate and mug at the kitchen sink. I slid down between the sheets, pulled my pillow under my head and was asleep by the time Malcolm closed the door behind himself.

★　★　★

I woke an hour or so later, but for a moment I had no idea what had woken me. Then I realized that the sound was the persistent whining of a dog. I sat up so suddenly in bed that my head started throbbing again. '*Oh God . . .* ' I murmured, shocked at my own thoughtlessness. It was Billy — but where was he? I had been so sorry for myself that I had not given him a thought when Malcolm brought me home. I tried to recall seeing him and could not even remember when I had last set eyes on the little fellow. Trying to keep my movements reasonably smooth I swung my legs over the side of the bed, felt for my slippers as I switched on the bedside lamp and made my way rather unsteadily across the room for my dressing-gown. Then I stood still and listened again. I jumped involuntarily when the whimpering was punctuated by a sharp bark that reverberated in my head and, to my sensitive ears, seemed to have an edge of hysteria to it.

Grabbing the large torch, which was more like a lantern, that I kept in my bedroom I made my way to the door. As I opened it a gust of wind nearly snatched it out of my grasp and a hairy projectile shot past my legs, giving the impression of having actually been blown inside. I pulled the door shut with difficulty against the force of the wind, turned the key and shot the bolt as quickly as I could. Only then did I look down at the little dog. Billy was shaking, his tail, normally a signal to the world of his cheerful spirit, was clamped between his legs and there was a muddy patch on his rump. When I touched it he gave a little whimper, confirming my suspicion that it was the mark of a muddy boot or shoe.

Heedless of the dirt on his coat I swept him up in my arms and held him close. Gradually the trembling stopped; I felt a slight vibration against my arm as his tail began its normal wagging and when I bent my head towards him a large pink tongue came out and licked my cheek. Crushed by guilt in the face of such forgiveness I leant my face against his rough, damp coat.

'Oh Billy . . . ' I crooned, 'I am so sorry — so very sorry — did I forget to let you in?' I put him down on the floor and turned towards the tiny kitchen area, intending to find some milk for him. Then I stopped in my tracks. 'Hey, wait a minute. I didn't put you out so I didn't forget you.' *No,* I thought to myself, *that isn't really an excuse: the truth is I was so sorry for myself I didn't give the poor little dog a thought.* 'You haven't even been fed this evening, have you?' I said to him. 'Come on, let's see what there is in the fridge.'

As I watched him demolish his food with gusto I realized that Malcolm must have put him outside when he brought me home and fussed over me. I was quite sure that I had not left him outside. Even allowing for a bump on the head I was convinced that I would never do a thing like that. I had come to look on my self-imposed task of caring for the little dog as something I owed to Grace. Also, as I had to admit to myself, he was company and it was better living with a dog than entirely alone.

When I went back to my bedroom I put an old blanket on the end of my bed and though he was soon snoring happily and loudly enough for me to find it necessary to prod him with my foot, sleep did not come easily a second time. My bedside clock told me it was nearly thirty minutes past midnight. I had in fact slept for an hour or so but there was still a lot of night to get through. I wondered if I should take another Panadol but the thought of getting out of bed again now that I was more or less warm and snug was off-putting. I tried to think when I had last seen Billy and could not remember if I had seen him inside when Malcolm brought me home. Was it possible I had put him outside before I went out and had then forgotten to let him in? Or had he followed Derek when he left, and got shut out? Common sense told me that that was unlikely, for Derek had left through the bathroom window. I was still trying to work it out in my mind when I dropped off to sleep and spent the remainder of the night in a series of garbled dreams; a mishmash of all the events of the last few days. Grace swam in and out of these dreams and when I woke I had the feeling that there was something I was missing — something I should know.

I got up feeling more confused than I had done since my aunt's untimely and shocking death. A glance at the clock told me that I had overslept and even missed the alarm going off. For almost the first time since I had been employed in the bookshop I felt loath to go in. I would, I decided, phone Tom and say I was sick and spend the day studying the package I had picked up from the lawyer's office.

My head still throbbed with a low dull ache and my mouth felt dry. A cup of tea, hot, strong and sweet was what I needed. I switched the kettle on then let Billy out to do what he had to do while it boiled. A glance at the time made me pick up my phone and, walking over to the window to make sure no one kidnapped Billy while I was on the phone, I called the shop. I was surprised to find Tom tetchy instead of his urbane self.

'I'm sorry,' I repeated, 'but I really don't feel up to coming in this morning. I guess everything has just caught up with me. I'll be in tomorrow.'

'I hope you will.' He sounded curt but added before I hung up, 'Well, look after yourself anyway.'

I was thoughtful as I let Billy safely back indoors and made myself a whole pot of tea. A teabag in a cup just wouldn't cut it this morning; I put the pot on a small tray with a peach and a banana and carried it back to the bedroom, where I placed them on the bedside table. I had decided to read the contents of the package from the lawyer over my breakfast.

Where on earth was it? Surely I had left it on the small table? Maybe on the kitchen counter, or perhaps I had taken it into the bedroom with me last night? There was no sign of it in any of these places. Could it have fallen on the floor, ended up under the bed? When a fairly extensive search of the whole flat failed to locate it I climbed back into bed with a puzzled frown, pulled up the pillows behind me so that I could sit upright and gratefully sipped my tea. I peeled the banana and bit into it still trying to remember what I had done with the envelope the previous evening. Surely the knock my head had received hadn't been bad enough to obliterate the memory of where I had put it?

Absently I picked up the small knife off the tray, removed the stone from my peach and cut the fruit into neat sections, but I was scarcely aware of eating it as I concentrated on my actions the previous evening. It all seemed a confused blur and the only thought I could dredge up about the package was that I must surely have put it somewhere safe.

I drained my teacup and decided the only thing to do was to get up and make an even more exhaustive manual search of my flat as looking for the envelope in my mind was proving so spectacularly unsuccessful. There was always the hope that if my brain couldn't remember where I had put it my body might.

When half an hour of intensive hunting in every possible, and impossible, place failed to turn it up I was ready to sit down and bawl my eyes out. I looked at Billy. Could he possibly have taken it? No, that was a ridiculous idea, but someone else could have done. Malcolm perhaps? He had expressed curiosity about it, but that didn't mean he had deliberately taken it. I cursed myself for last night's muzzy head that seemed to have robbed me of memory. It seemed the only course left was to call Malcolm on the phone and ask him outright if he had taken it when he left.

Another caffeine fix seemed called for

while I worked out the best way to approach the problem. This time I made myself a good strong cup of coffee, the tea had been delicious and reviving but it hadn't done much to sharpen my wits. I pulled up a stool to the counter and pulled the mug close. I had made it so strong it needed two spoonfuls of sugar to make it palatable. I stirred it automatically and tried to string the right words together in my head before I rang Malcolm. It would be difficult to accuse him baldly of making off with my personal and private property after he had been so kind and caring when he brought me home.

I was in the shower, still planning how I would broach the subject, when I heard the phone over the sound of the water. Convinced it was Malcolm I turned off the taps, wrapped myself in a large bath sheet and hurried to answer, putting together what I would say as I went. It must be just as I had thought: he had the missing package and wanted to return it.

The only thing was, it was not Malcolm but Derek on the line.

9

'Derek! Sorry to be so long answering — I was in the shower when I heard the phone . . . ' Thrown off balance I heard myself gabbling and hoped he wouldn't think my breathlessness was caused by hearing his voice.

'How are you this morning? Much, much better, I hope, with no permanent bumps and lumps on your head.' He sounded as if he cared and I warmed towards him.

'Better, thanks. You could say I still look a bit battered — the morning after the night before sort of thing, so I decided to have a day off work and give my bruises time to fade.'

'Good — good. No, I don't mean good that you are bruised and battered — good that you are at home. I mean — well, you probably need a day at least to recover.' Now he was the one trying to fill the silence with pointless words. His voice trailed off and I waited without speaking for an explanation. I was not very pleased when it came.

'I thought you would be at the bookshop so I have taken it there.'

'What do you mean, Derek? What are you talking about? What have you left at the bookshop?' I was not certain I had heard him correctly having already decided that it was Malcolm who was responsible for the envelope's disappearance.

'I'm talking about that package of yours — you know, the big A4 envelope obviously stuffed full of papers. I didn't mean to but somehow I picked it up when I left last night. Can't think how.' I couldn't figure out quite how he could do that and apparently also not realize he had done it. It was difficult to believe that it was a genuine mistake.

'Not to worry,' I said airily; better if no one suspected it might be important until I had had a chance to read the contents of the envelope myself. 'I don't suppose there is anything in it of great importance; probably only copies of old bills or something equally dreary.' I hoped I was not overdoing the idea that there was nothing in the envelope of interest not to only to me, but to the police and perhaps a sticky-nosed journalist. 'I will pop round and get it now.'

'Didn't you hear what I said? I've left it at the shop. I didn't like to disturb you too early this morning so I put it in the car with the intention of giving it to you when you were at work. Of course I found you were not at work

111

so I left it there. I was going to bring it back home with me and come round and give it to you personally, but . . . ' He paused and I thought I heard him sigh, whether in frustration or irritation or a mixture of both I wasn't sure.

'But?' I prompted, trying to keep the anxiety and impatience out of my voice.

'Well that is what I *intended* to do, but the old guy in the shop — what's his name — Ensley — '

'Tom Ensley — he owns it,' I supplied.

'Well, yes — whatever — he said it was silly for me to take it away — much better to leave it with him as you would be in soon. You were just a bit late this morning and he would give it to you. Sounded reasonable enough, I thought, so that's what I did.'

'What time were you there?'

'A few minutes ago, I've only just left, I am in the car ringing you on my mobile.'

If he had only just left it, then Tom had already spoken to me and knew I did not intend going into the shop. Yet he had allowed Derek to think I would be. Odd — and a little disturbing.

'Why did you bother ringing me if you thought I would be in the shop shortly?'

'To tell you the truth I don't really know. I just began to wonder if leaving it there had

112

been the right thing to do, and now I find you are not going to work I am even less sure I did right.'

'Oh, don't worry about it,' I began wearily; it seemed I was to be forever thwarted in my attempts to find out what was so special about the unpublished manuscript in the envelope and why my aunt had left it to me anyway. 'I expect I will get it eventually — it's just that — well, I thought I would read it while I was home this morning. Thanks anyway.' Replacing the receiver with a faint sense of irritation I wondered what I was bothering to thank him for. The wretched man had taken my property — a likely story that it was accidental — and handed it over to someone else.

Remembering that I was only wearing a bath towel I went to dress, wondering what on earth had Grace written in the typescript, and why everyone wanted to get hold of it and read it before I could? Honesty forced me to admit that I had no evidence that other people actually wanted to inspect the contents. It was my own fault for not looking after it better. But I couldn't help wondering why Tom had told Derek he would give it to me when I came in later that morning when I had clearly said I wasn't going into the shop at all that day. But that was because I planned to read whatever was in that damn envelope. Thwarted in my intention and feeling considerably stronger, I would go into the shop after all, if only to collect it.

It was a clear, cool morning when Billy and I set off on the short walk to the shop. I found my head clearing in the fresh air, so I really did feel much better. I went in the back way to drop Billy off. Tom looked up from the catalogue he was studying, apparently unsurprised to see me. 'Hope you put the kettle on as you came through — I'm ready for my elevenses,' was all he said.

I hadn't, but after a quick glance round the shop and noting that there were three customers browsing the shelves and a fourth just coming up to the counter, I hurried to comply, deciding at the same time that as things seemed busy I had better stay. Tom dealt with the woman at the counter, who left with several books in her shopping-bag. Then he turned to me and slapped his hand down on a familiar package on his desk.

'Young man brought this in and left it here. Said he picked it up by mistake when he left your place last night.' He raised his eyebrow and his expression said *Likely story*.

'That's quite true; he phoned me a short while ago and said it was here.' I picked it up, feeling an absurd desire to hug it to my bosom like a lost child I had been reunited with, but I controlled the impulse and stowed it safely with my bag and outdoor clothes. I had let it go physically for the time being but it still occupied my thoughts. Even though I had told myself I was being quite neurotic about the thing I couldn't quite dismiss the notion that too many people seemed unduly interested in the contents of the mysterious package.

By mid-afternoon the events of the last few days caught up on me. I sighed and flopped down in the big armchair in the shop; it was there for the use of those customers who liked to browse thoroughly before buying. For the best part of an hour I had been kept busy by a demanding customer searching for this book and that. At least, I thought thankfully, he had eventually left with a bulging bag.

Tom peered at me over the top of his reading-glasses. 'You look dreadful,' he said bluntly. 'Make yourself a cup of tea then go home. Better still — go home and then make yourself a cup of tea. That way you can't be anchored here by another customer like the last.' He seemed to have forgotten that I wasn't supposed to be there at all.

I managed a somewhat lopsided grin. 'Gee, thanks for the compliment; you sure know how to make a girl feel great. But yes — you are right — I feel dreadful, kinda wiped out, so if you are sure you can cope I will go.'

When I left a few minutes later I made sure the envelope was in my bag, a capacious and shabby old thing that I clung to because it held so much. With Billy's lead securely snapped to his collar I stuck my head in through the back of the shop and called 'goodbye' to Tom, I had to say it twice; he was in a world of his own, staring into space, not at the catalogues and columns of figures on the desk in front of him. I wondered why on earth he didn't learn to use a computer; surely it would make life so much easier for him. But his answer was always the same — with second-hand books it was not necessary to keep track of them in the same way as in a retail shop dealing in new books. It seemed a very flawed argument to me and I suspected the real reason was that he couldn't face the effort it would take to make himself computer literate.

Once home I flicked on the electric kettle and flopped down in my most comfortable chair, still in my outdoor clothes. I flung my bag down on the small table at my side. Then, with a weary sigh, I got up to take off my coat and make myself a pot of tea, absently admiring, as I did nearly every time I used it, the small china teapot I had picked up in a thrift shop. It held about two and a half mugs of tea or three smaller cups and I always found something soothing in simply pouring from it, rather than extracting a soggy tea bag from the liquid. I poured a cup and feeling more relaxed than I had since I got up leaned back in my chair to enjoy it. My eyes fell on that damn envelope and I decided to drink my tea first. After which I might feel strong enough to face the contents.

When I eventually opened the large bulky envelope I wondered why I was so convinced that the contents would need facing, there was also the possibility that they might be cheering and uplifting — and God knows that was what I needed at the moment.

Nothing had changed since I last looked inside the envelope. At least that was my first impression. I wondered if I had been mistaken in thinking this was the script of a novel; it was probably Grace's autobiography. Then I saw the name on the title page and remembered it had not been Grace Arbuth-not but Faith Treloar. Someone — was it the solicitor? — had said something about Grace giving Faith Treloar to me. *But how could you give another person to anyone.* I mused wearily, as I pulled the sheaf of typescript in a clear plastic sleeve out of the large envelope. I frowned; it didn't look quite the same as the last time I had seen it. It took a few moments' concentration before I remembered that there had been a single-sheet letter with my name on it on top of the pile. It was no longer there.

I asked myself if I were going slightly mad; I seemed to be forever searching for objects that had disappeared. *No, I told myself sternly, I was not going mad but all the other people in my world were definitely not as sane as they should be.* Hard on the heels of this thought came another and I laughed aloud, genuinely amused, and at myself, for the first time in days. I was thinking like the doting mother who, watching the passing-out parade of her son at military college, turned to her husband and said, 'Look Dad, they are all out of step but our Johnny!' This was such a Grace-like saying that I gulped and my laughter nearly turned to tears.

If only, I thought, Grace were here, I would know what to do. But that, I knew, was totally impossible and if it had been possible then Grace would still be alive and none of this would have arisen. It was with this thought that the actual loss of my aunt, as distinct from the fact of her murder, really struck home. I knew I was going to miss her terribly. She had always been such a fount of good advice, all given with her particular brand of sardonic humour. Thinking like this reminded me that I was very much alone in the world. With Grace's death I had lost the person whom I believed to be my only living relative.

I thought back to the time when my parents died and Grace had appeared from out of the blue and taken me — an angry and frightened child, all prickles and defiance — home with her. I remembered the years that followed, which she had filled with love and security, her advice and guidance always available. With her death all that had gone and I felt as lonely and — yes — afraid as I had as a small child.

At one time I had hoped to join Grace in her antiques shop. But it had been firmly pointed out to me by my aunt that there was nowhere near enough work for two and even less sufficient income. Always interested in old things, I had worked briefly in a renowned auction house that specialized in antiques. Even though I had only worked on the secretarial side it had still given me an opportunity to see, even occasionally handle, fine old things and to learn something of their value. This was when I began to wonder how Grace made a living from her business.

When that job folded up I had suggested again that I might help Grace, but was told again that there was not enough work for two of us. But when it was suggested that I might enjoy working in a bookshop which dealt in old and rare books as well as run-of-the-mill second-hand ones, and a vacancy arose in Tom's, I jumped at the chance and in my heart agreed with Grace that it was better for me to be independent in my own space than for the two of us to share Grace's small flat. That was when she offered me my present flat at a ridiculously low rent.

I rather drifted into my relationship with Malcolm. I had told Grace on the night of my birthday dinner with her that I thought he might ask me to marry him. I had been somewhat taken aback at Grace's lack of enthusiasm or encouragement. 'Have a fling by all means if you feel you must,' she had advised, 'but think very hard before you commit yourself to anything serious.'

I was mulling over her words and musing that even the idea of a fling with Malcolm had lost its appeal over the last few days when the phone rang.

'Josh Smethurst here from Smethurst, Smethurst & Smethurst,' said a crisp professional voice in my ear.

'Ah, yes, Mr Smethurst.'

'As you are aware, we are Grace Arbuthnot's solicitors and the executors of her will.'

He paused and cleared his throat.

'Yes, Mr Smethurst, I am aware of that — can I help you?' I said politely into the pause.

'I have just phoned you to ask about funeral arrangements for Miss Arbuthnot. The police will release the — er — body in a week or two and have given permission for arrangements to be — er — made.' He seemed to be having trouble, I thought, actually coming to terms with the fact that his client was dead. Or maybe his problem was in discussing it with me.

'Yes?' I waited for him to tell me why he was calling.

'Well as you are — er — the next of kin I assume you will wish to consider the funeral arrangements, Miss — er — Divine.'

'But I didn't think I was the next of kin — I mean — well, I always thought I was, then the police told me that Grace — er — Miss Arbuthnot's stepson had identified the body. I hadn't known she had a stepson.'

'A stepson, no blood relation.'

'Does this mean I have to make the arrangements?' I was stumbling over my words now. The only response from the other end of the line for what seemed a long minute was silence.

'The thing is, Miss Divine, although we

121

have received a few suggestions the consensus is that you should have the final say-so. If you could think about it and let me know what you wish I will — er — help you make the arrangements.'

I was appalled. My voice came out small, weak and helpless when I pleaded, 'Couldn't you — I mean your firm — as my aunt's executors, make the arrangements?'

'We will do all we can to help you over things like religion, any preferences she may have expressed, or that you may have.'

She had not been very religious. I had never known her go to a church of any denomination for anything other than what she called *hatches, matches and dispatches*. I murmured vaguely that I supposed she was C of E; it seemed safest and all I could remember her saying about funerals was that they should be cheerful, not morbid, if those left behind really believed people went to a better place.

'Quite, quite. I — see.' He sounded unconvinced and I was left with the impression that he found me both unhelpful and frivolous. 'Well — we shall just have to do our best.' I thought he was referring to Smethurst, Smethurst & Smethurst handling it themselves until he added: 'If you would like help call into my office and we can discuss it.'

I agreed and hung up. How come, I wondered, that in all the harrowing hassles of Grace's death it had not occurred to me that there would have to be a funeral? And what about this mysterious stepson who had sprung up from nowhere? Where was he now?

10

'Ah — good morning Miss Divine. So glad you could come.' Josh Smethurst indicated the seat opposite him and I obediently sat. Of course I was here; his suggestion that I should come and see him had been in the nature of a royal command. 'I am assuming that you are not particularly in favour of a very large funeral in the — er — the circumstances?'

Feeling much more like myself this morning I saw no merit in what I thought of as pussyfooting around. 'Are you referring to the fact that my aunt was murdered, or suggesting she did not have a wide circle of friends and relations who would wish to attend her funeral?'

'Well, I suppose both.' He looked up from the papers he was studying, met my stern gaze and smiled. It was so sudden and unexpected that I smiled back. He slid a sheet of paper across the desk to me. 'These are my preliminary plans. Tell me if you think they would be in order. Did Miss Arbuthnot ever express a wish for anything special — cremation, for instance?'

'This seems fine to me,' I approved, as I

scanned his notes. 'We never discussed her death so I never knew if she had any preferences. She wasn't one to dwell on the morbid.'

'I am afraid most of us tend to think we are immortal,' Josh Smethurst murmured. 'But she must have considered the possibility that she was not when she made a will. Some years ago in fact. Then she changed it quite recently.'

Grace had never discussed either her will or her funeral. It would have been easier if she had.

There seemed little point in doing anything other than to accede to the suggested arrangements that Josh had outlined for Grace's funeral. It would commence at eleven on the appointed day and the hearse would take Grace to the local cemetery where the local vicar would conduct the ceremony. I agreed with him that Grace would not appreciate a eulogy, chiefly because I was petrified at the prospect of being asked to give it.

'Just one thing Miss Divine . . . ' I had reached the door when Josh Smethurst spoke. I turned back in surprise.

'Yes?'

'The package your aunt left in our safe-keeping for you — you have it?'

I nodded. 'Yes, I have.'

'Have you had time to read it?'

'Not in depth as yet. I intend to as soon as — well, as soon as I can settle down to it.'

'But you will have read the covering letter, of course?' In spite of the casual way he spoke I got the impression that the question was loaded and that he was almost holding his breath for my answer.

I murmured vaguely in the affirmative, feeling it was too melodramatic to say anything about it being stolen, but casually said I had mislaid it.

He stared at me with a worried frown. 'Could it have got in to the pile of papers, lost its place on top?'

'I — I really don't know. I wouldn't have thought so, but I suppose it is possible. Is it important?'

He frowned. 'I think it may be. Please have a good look for it and let me know as soon as you find it — please.' The last word was tagged on as if he had suddenly remembered his manners. I had the feeling that he was about to insist that I rush home to start a thorough search immediately, but he just stared at me, concern etched on his face. At last, with a heavy sigh, he reached a hand across his desk to me. 'Goodbye, Miss Divine.' The time for a friendlier approach was gone. 'Thank you for coming in this morning. I shall see you when we meet to lay Miss Arbuthnot to rest. If I don't hear from you before.'

I suppressed a smile. I thought Josh Smethurst talked as if he had walked out of a Dickens novel. All the same, there was something about him I both liked and trusted.

'Goodbye, Mr Smethurst.' I had nearly said I would look forward to seeing him, but it didn't seem quite appropriate when the forthcoming meeting was to be at a funeral.

* * *

'You are very late this morning.' I was taken aback by this curt greeting from Tom. The apology I had framed in my mind almost died on my lips.

'I'm sorry. I should have phoned you and explained that I might be a little late. I had to see Mr Smethurst about the arrangements for Grace's funeral.'

'And why should he have anything to do with it?'

'He, that is Smethurst, Smethurst & Smethurst, are the executors of Grace's will.'

'I should have thought it would have been up to her relatives to make all the arrangements.'

'That is why Josh Smethurst wanted to see me,' I explained, feeling my patience stretching under what was fast becoming a cross-examination.

'What about the mysterious stepson who, according to the police, identified her?'

'He is so mysterious no one seems to know where he is,' I replied, my voice sharper than I intended. I had been removing my outdoor clothes as we talked. Now I added, 'What would you like me to do first?' in a tone that deliberately returned us to the status of employer and employee in the hope that that would get him off my back about Grace and her official send-off.

'Oh, go and play with that computer of yours; see if you can make sense of the accounts, I'm having no luck,' he told me pettishly, as he pushed the pile of papers on his desk to one side.

'You never can,' I muttered under my breath. I smiled to myself. It had been a difficult task persuading him when I first came to work in the shop that even a bookshop dealing in old books needed to move with the times and invest in a computer system. He himself steadfastly refused to have anything to do with it, struggling with the accounts in the same way as he had done for years while I dealt with them on the

128

computer. I had given up trying to convince him that he was wasting his time. I had also put in long hours and had even won a grunt of reluctant appreciation when I had been able to tell him that we had a book in stock that he wanted, without the need to do a physical search for it.

Unlike him I loved computers and was usually more than happy to spend time 'playing with my new toy' as Tom enjoyed saying. Today I found it hard to keep my mind and my attention on my work. Only a week ago everything had seemed normal — almost serene — in my own particular world. Now with Grace's sudden and brutal death it had become a chaotic nightmare.

11

It was almost impossible to concentrate on anything as mundane as accounts with my mind swirling with thoughts of Grace's untimely death and the added mystery of the man who claimed to be her stepson who appeared and disappeared again more like a will-o-the-wisp than a real live flesh-and-blood person. I wished I knew something, anything about this so-called stepson of my aunt's, who he was, and where he came from, and, above all, where he was now. He must, I supposed, have produced some credentials or proof of identity to convince the police that he was who he said he was. But why had he vanished again?

I tried desperately to drag my attention back to the computer and the wretched task of sorting out the accounts; the job would be a great deal easier, I reflected rather sourly, if only Tom would leave it entirely to me. Instead he constantly bombarded me with sheets of paper covered in figures written in a hand that looked as if a spider in hobnailed boots on all eight feet had walked across the paper. However hard I tried to concentrate I could not put out of my mind that in a week or two my beloved aunt would be buried. Absurdly I wished Grace could be there to help me get through the day; a thought that brought home the truth: Grace would never again be there to bolster my determination when it flagged, or to give advice, always getting to the real crux of any problem. Grace was dead and I had to accept it, just as a child I had been forced to square up to the reality that I would never see my parents again. Grace had come to my rescue then; this time there was no one. My hands lay still on the keyboard and my eyes, misted with tears. I couldn't see to work, so I gave up; there was no way I could bring my mind to bear on accounts today. I was staring blankly into space when, through my misery, I heard the shop door behind me open. I turned round. Tom was standing in the doorway of the little back room we called the office staring at me, the glumness of his expression a mirror of my own feelings, but with something else which for some reason caused a shiver to run up my spine. I gave myself a mental shake. Of course he was upset — he and Grace had known one another for a long time.

'You never told me exactly what arrangements have been made to send Grace on her way.'

I smiled inwardly at his choice of words and imagined Grace telling him she was not catching a train and, as far as she was concerned, they could put her in the compost.

'I think she would be quite satisfied with the arrangements. She was never one for ceremony.' I wondered why we avoided the word funeral.

'No doubt. But you still haven't told me just what you and that solicitor fellow decided on.'

'I'm sorry — I really am — I should have told you as soon as I came in.' I felt really contrite as I turned round on my chair and quickly explained what had been decided.

'Hrrumph.' His grunt was noncommittal. 'What about refreshments?'

'Refreshments?' I repeated blankly. 'What about them?'

'It's normal to offer refreshments. People who attend a funeral expect some recompense for showing their respect.'

I was mortified; I simply hadn't given the matter a thought. Why hadn't that solicitor or someone mentioned it?

Tom shrugged. 'I don't suppose there will be more than a handful of people there anyway. Those who are will need some sort of lunch so we can always get together and have a snack somewhere. The shop will be closed for the day.' His lips twisted into a wry smile. 'I might find I need a liquid lunch,' he added.

★　★　★

I was surprised to see several people at the church when Tom and I arrived. I had obviously been cast in the role of chief mourner, and I was conscious of the curious but not unsympathetic glances as I walked up the aisle. I wished I could have crept into the back of the church just an anonymous mourner. I was kneeling, looking as if I was praying, when a movement made me screw round slightly. Malcolm had slipped in beside me. I smiled my thanks for his support and wondered if one of the other men in the church could be Grace's stepson. I also wondered about the murderer. I had read somewhere that killers could seldom resist attending their victims' funerals. In the churchyard I had recognized the police detective assigned to the case; everything else was blurred. Later at the graveside I saw the detective again and this time I recognized Derek standing close to him. Josh Smethurst was there too, among a few familiar faces.

I shuddered as the coffin was lowered into the grave and had to suppress a wild urge to yell at Grace to stop being silly and get out of that damn box at once. When Tom stepped forward I even thought for one crazy moment that he was going to let her out, but he snatched the white carnation from his lapel and threw it on to the coffin. It landed on the top fractionally ahead of the first symbolic shovelful of soil. When I had first seen him wearing it I thought he looked more like a wedding guest than someone at a funeral. Now I understood, or thought I did. The clergyman was solemnly intoning the bit about 'earth to earth'. I tried to switch off.

'Just a moment!' My heart thumped when I felt a hand on my arm. My first thought was that I was under arrest. Malcolm was leading me to his car; there was only another yard to go and I would have been away.

'Yes?' My voice didn't sound as if it were coming from my own mouth. Glancing up into the policeman's face I saw only apologetic concern and relaxed somewhat.

He put his head closer to mine and asked in a low voice, little more than a whisper, 'I just wondered if there was anyone here that you recognized, Miss Divine? Perhaps you could take a quick glance around before everyone moves away.'

'Yes, there are local people here whom I

know by sight and, of course, some of my aunt's friends.'

'I meant someone — well, someone who might . . . ' His voice trailed away as if he himself was not quite sure just what he did mean.

'You think I might recognize her killer — is that what you are asking?' I tried to sound cool but was afraid I only sounded blunt, betraying how uptight I felt. Surely the wretched man could see that I was upset and that this was no time to be answering questions like that. 'No, I didn't see anyone, that is not anyone strange — not anyone I don't know even if only slightly.'

'I was just wondering . . . ' he persisted, when he was interrupted by a firm male voice. 'I don't think this is the time to question Miss Divine about anything; surely you can understand how she feels at the moment?' The firm hand on my elbow belonged to Malcolm but the voice was Derek's.

Discovering to my chagrin that I appeared to have lost the power of speech I nodded vaguely at the detective to confirm this.

'It was a long shot, I hoped you might have seen something, someone that might give us a lead. You are the last person we know who actually saw your aunt alive.' His voice was so low I barely caught the words.

I stared. Did he really suspect me of hiding information, or worse? The idea was bizarre; surely no one suspected me of having had anything to do with Grace's death?

'You will let me know if anything — any memory — comes back to you?'

His voice was soft but I noticed that the slight smile hovering round his mouth failed to reach his eyes.

I shook my head slightly as if to shake away the man's words and prove to myself that they had only been in my imagination. I stared after him as he turned on his heel and walked away, leaving me enclosed, as if for protection, by a small circle of men: Malcolm, who still held my arm, Derek who had, so surprisingly, come to my defence and Tom, who had moved away from the grave at last and joined them. It gave me a feeling of security, but it was a trifle claustrophobic.

12

'Miss Divine.' Sensing someone else moving into the group I turned and looked straight up into Josh Smethurst's face.

'Oh,' I gasped, surprised to see him, though why I couldn't say.

I was even more surprised when he asked, 'Would you care to have some lunch with me?'

'Well, I . . . ' I turned to Tom, but he was already moving away. 'You go on. I'm off to drown my sorrows.' Before I could protest he had gone. I shifted my gaze to Malcolm's face and was surprised to read his expression, definitely embarrassed but equally definitely relieved.

'That would be kind of you.' He was speaking to Josh. 'I have a business appointment.' I was more than a little miffed to be spoken about as though I were not there and handed over like some unwanted parcel. Instinctively I looked round for Derek, but all I could see was his back view walking away with the detective. No doubt sleuth-hounding again.

I turned back to Josh Smethurst, feeling

abandoned and suddenly, and surprisingly, hungry. 'Thank you,' I said, 'that is very kind of you.' Now, too late, I realized what a mistake it had been not to arrange for some sort of refreshments after the service.

We crossed the road to the Griffin Hotel, not only the nearest eating-place but possibly one of the best in the town. Its sombre atmosphere engendered by thick carpets, rather dark decoration and furniture and obsequious staff gave one the impression of being insulated from the outside world; it was, given the circumstances, entirely suitable. I settled in my chair and let the aura of timeless respectability enfold me. For the first time in days I felt relaxed, or possibly just relieved to have got through the morning. Feeling almost disconnected from my body I allowed my companion to choose from the menu and accepted without demur the glass of red wine he offered. It was an odd, surreal sensation, though certainly not unpleasant. Maybe it was the wine speaking when I looked straight across the table and asked, 'Did you know my aunt had a stepson?'

Josh Smethurst shook his head. 'I asked my father about him. As you know he was Grace Arbuthnot's solicitor for many years. I inherited her, as it were, when my father retired. He would have been here today

138

but . . . ' His voice trailed away. When he saw I was waiting for a further explanation he sighed and added, 'He died a few months ago.'

'I'm sorry.' I murmured. I was, truly; he might have been able to help. 'Did he know — about Grace's stepson I mean?'

'Well, yes and no.'

I arched my eyebrows at this answer. Surely it would be something one either knew or did not know. Josh smiled slightly at my expression.

'I know that sounds absurd, but what he told me was that Grace married a long time ago when she was living in Australia. I don't know what happened; I was very small at the time — probably not even in existence. He told me when I took over Grace's affairs. From what I gather the marriage did not last very long, only a few years.' It crossed my mind that in today's marriage climate a few years was quite a long time. 'He said she never talked about her time out of England so, respecting her wish for privacy, he never asked about it. Did she ever mention it to you?'

I shook my head. 'Until this week I never heard Australia mentioned in connection with Grace. She must have been very determined to put her past firmly behind her when she left Australia.' A flash of annoyance with my secretive aunt made me sigh. 'So it is possible she did have a stepson, but for some reason he remained in Australia.' I shook my head as another thought struck me. 'I don't ever remember letters coming from or going to Australia.' The thought that Grace could have a stepson and have nothing whatsoever to do with him seemed so unlike what I knew of her that I shook my head.

'She was so good to me when I needed someone that I cannot imagine she would abandon anyone.' I sipped my wine slowly, lost in thought. 'But then, if what you say is true, who identified my aunt — after — after . . . ?' My voice shook as I remembered again the appalling truth of how my poor aunt had met her death. I blinked hard, took a large gulp of wine and almost choked.

Josh looked concerned for a moment saying, with a resigned acceptance that I admired and was repelled by at the same time, 'We have little alternative but to accept that Miss Arbuthnot's body was identified by her stepson. The fact that you and I did not know about him does not mean there is no such person.' Spoken like a lawyer, I thought, but I said nothing. He continued; 'You realize of course . . . '

I braced myself to hear once again that I was the last person known to have seen Grace alive. As I was about to protest at what, each time I heard it, sounded more like an accusation to my sensitive ears, I looked up and saw over my companion's shoulder, Derek threading his way towards another table.

After that I was conscious all the time of Derek's presence somewhere behind me in the restaurant and longed to turn round and see if he was, as I felt, watching me. I tried hard to make some sort of intelligent, if not bright, conversation, but it was hard going for Josh's replies were for the most part monosyllabic. I had the feeling that he had invited me to lunch out of a mistaken sense of duty.

We had barely finished our lunch when I saw him glancing surreptitiously at his watch.

Before he could say anything I jumped in with, 'Well, I had better be going. Thanks very much for the lunch.'

He smiled then. 'Yes, I am afraid I have to get back to the office. I have appointments this afternoon.'

He paid the bill and we walked out on to the pavement together. He seemed much more at ease with me now the moment of parting had come. 'Thank you,' he said, taking my hand. I wasn't quite sure what I was being thanked for but smiled graciously. 'If you have any problems, get in touch. In the meantime I'll be working on your aunt's estate and will contact you when I have sorted things out.'

I murmured more thanks and we went our separate ways.

A few seconds later I heard footsteps behind me and, as I turned, a hand gripped my arm.

'Derek!' I exclaimed, annoyed with myself for being startled — and showing it. 'What do you want?' I demanded ungraciously.

'Just to walk with you to the shop.'

'I'm not going to the shop. Tom has closed it for the whole day.'

'Then I'll walk with you back home — or wherever.'

'I don't need looking after.'

'No,' he agreed, 'but I like doing it.'

Something in his voice, or the admission deep down that I *did* need looking after, caught me by the throat and try as I would I was unable to stop laughter tinged with hysteria and perilously near to tears. This inevitably slowed my pace and taking advantage of this Derek was at my side again.

'Just tell me, calmly and reasonably, what you have so much against me?'

I threw a sideways glance at him and tried to remember what it was about him that had so annoyed me. 'You — well — you are too much of a sticky beak.' Was all I could find to say.

'I'm a journalist.'

'Maybe I don't like reporters, people who earn their living prying into other people's business.' I knew I sounded unbearably prim, smug almost, and hated it. I kept on walking and willed myself not to turn my head and look at him, but curiosity got the better of me; after all two could play the sticky-beak game. 'Why did you decide to lunch in the same restaurant?' I demanded.

'I thought maybe it was the official wake. People at funerals usually get supplied with nibbles at least.'

'Yes,' I agreed, feeling uncomfortable. 'Well, there was no official wake as you refer to it at this funeral.' By this time we had reached my flat. Derek positioned himself in front of my gate in such a way that I could not get in without physically pushing him out of the way.

'Please move out of the way and let me get to my door . . . ' I heard the rising hysteria in my own voice in stark contrast to Derek's reasonable tone.

'How about asking me in for a cup of

coffee, tea or whatever, and we can talk calmly?'

I glared at him for a moment. 'Oh, all right then. On condition you explain to me why you are behaving in such an odd way.' I was painfully aware that I sounded thoroughly disgruntled and that the invitation was ungracious, but anything, I thought, was better than this undignified wrangle out in the street.

Once through the door Billy gave us both a rapturous welcome. To my chagrin I thought he showed even more enthusiasm for Derek than for myself. 'Tea or coffee?' I almost spat the words.

'Coffee, please.'

'Black or white?'

'Black — one sugar,' he snapped back in such a wicked imitation of myself that I fought to keep my smile at bay.

When I added in much the same peremptory tone, 'Sit down!' and Billy dropped his butt to the floor I was in danger of laughing out loud.

'I meant you.' I was glad of an excuse to turn away to make the promised coffee. 'Billy likes you,' I conceded, as I turned back and saw the little dog curled up near Derek's feet and that he, too, was now obediently seated on the sofa.

Remembering that I was not really his mistress; I added, 'He was Grace's dog. He must miss her and — and feel lost.' I tried to control the wobble in my voice.

'Yes, it is hard on animals when the person they love dies.' Derek bent to stroke the little dog's head. I watched Billy's reaction and wondered if dogs really were better judges of character than people. Billy looked on Derek with a far kinder eye than I did, but what did he really see?

'You can keep your side of the bargain now and explain to me why you are so interested in this whole awful business,' I said as I handed Derek his coffee.

'I've told you — I'm a journalist.'

'Yes, you have told me, several times, but you haven't told me what paper or magazine or radio programme or whatever you represent.'

'I am a freelance. Working for myself.'

'But why such an interest in this case?'

'My main concern is with you; I don't want to see anything happen to you.'

'Why on earth should it?' In spite of myself I felt a *frisson* of alarm ripple down my spine. 'Because I was the last person to see her alive? You think the police have me on the top of their list of suspects?' I expected him to laugh that off as nonsense. But he didn't.

'That, yes. But I think you are in danger — you may know too much for your own safety.'

'I was the last person to see her alive, granted. To be honest, that worried me too, but to say I know too much is absurd. I know nothing — absolutely nothing. What makes you think I do?'

'You have that typescript of your aunt's last book. I think the secret of what brought about her death could be in its pages.'

'Oh, Derek! You are the one who should be writing books — thrillers — I have had a quick flip through the manuscript and it is just more of the same sort of thing she had written before, just another pleasant little love story. That, apparently, is what Grace specialized in and she had a reasonable following, especially in the libraries, so that her books sold enough for the public to want another one all the time and so make her financially independent of that shop of hers. I never could work out how she made a living from it. She liked to call it an antiques shop but honestly, junk shop would have been more appropriate.'

Derek listened to my spiel before shrugging slightly in a gesture that was both expressive and irritating. 'Have it your own way, but all the same, if I were you I would read that manuscript very carefully indeed.' He sprang to his feet. 'Now I must love you and leave you. Remember, if you need any help I am only just the other side of that fence.'

I jumped up to see him out and found myself standing face to face with him in the limited space. For a second we stared at each other, eyeball to eyeball, then he put a hand on each of my shoulders, leaned towards me and kissed me swiftly on the cheek. 'Don't forget if anything, anything at all bothers you, sing out for me. And Angie, please — take care!'

Then he turned and almost before I realized what he was doing let himself out. I continued to stand there, feeling . . . I am not quite sure what I was feeling. The fingers of my right hand absently stroked my cheek where he had kissed me. Billy stared at the door, the faint quiver in his tail asking why Derek had left so suddenly.

13

'Billy,' I confided, 'I am more than bemused, I am totally confused.' I glossed over the fact that I was also, deep down, more than a little worried. I didn't need anyone to remind me that I was the last person who had seen my aunt alive, other than the murderer. Suppose the police really did suspect me? My only alibi was Grace, who was the victim. I had been with her all her last evening alive but the only person who knew that and could testify to it was Grace herself. But Grace was dead, murdered by some person or persons unknown.

I walked across to the electric kettle and flicked it on, I needed to think and a good cup of tea in my experience always helped thought as well as soothing nerves. I remembered that Derek had come in for that very purpose, a cup of tea or coffee. Somehow it hadn't materialized, so I would make up for it and have one on my own. While I drank it I would read Grace's manuscript, if only to satisfy Derek who was convinced I would find information hidden in its pages.

I remembered ruefully how I had sworn to myself after my last, disastrous personal relationship had ended in the discovery that Tony was not just married, but much married, that I would never get embroiled with a man again. Grace had encouraged me to come back here to the little country town where I had spent most of my childhood. By offering me my own place to live she had given me a new life, for the second time. The example she set before me of doing her own thing had convinced me that a single life like hers was the free and independent way I wanted to spend my own life.

At this point my reminiscing pulled up short with the painful realization that Grace's life had apparently been far from uncomplicated and her ending anything but peaceful. I shuddered and added an extra teabag to my little teapot before I poured on the boiling water. I suppressed the niggling reminder that my own life was now in danger of becoming complicated, even dangerous. Not only was I probably the prime suspect in a murder case but I, who had sworn to forsake all men, was now involved with a whole army of them; that was, if you counted Josh Smethurst and Tom as well as Malcolm and Derek, and that was not mentioning this mysterious stepson of Grace, who, I supposed was some sort of cousin.

I sat down with my pot of tea and collected the package of papers, Grace's last book, which Derek had suggested could be the key to the mystery of why she had been killed. To me the idea was far-fetched, but as Grace had left me the copyright in her books maybe it was not such a bad idea to learn something about them. I had glanced through the published ones in the shop, but as far as I could see, they were nothing more than straightforward romances.

This one appeared to be more of the same. Just a pleasant light novel. The most surprising thing to me about her books was they were so totally unlike the sort of books I had seen Grace read that I found it hard to imagine, let alone believe, that they were written by her. Grace had always been one to speak her mind, and not in sentimental platitudes but with a wit that was sharp to the point of being acid. I had found it awesome, in the true sense of the word. Yet this had been the spice she added to her very wise, sensible and down-to-earth advice when asked for help on a problem. The pages of her books, were sweet to the point of being syrupy, including this unpublished script in which I was now immersing myself. And yet there was something that kept me reading. However sentimental the story there was that indefinable 'something' about the way Grace told it that made me keep reading. That, or Derek's conviction that there was something of interest hidden in the pages.

By the time I had drained my little teapot at least some of the tangles had been teased out of my fraught nerves; how much was due to the tea and how much to the novel I was reading I couldn't be sure, but I was more than ready to succumb to the weariness engendered by the emotions of the day. It became hard to keep my mind on what I was reading; my eyelids drooped and the hand holding the sheaf of papers dropped to my lap, my fingers loosed their grip and the manuscript fell in a heap of untidy papers around my feet.

It was Billy's shrill warning yap, not the doorbell itself, which roused me. It took a few moments for me to marshal my wits and register that it was still afternoon and I was not asleep in my bed and even longer to gather up the scattered papers into some semblance of order. I cursed under my breath as the bell pealed again while I was putting them as neatly as possible on the coffee table in front of me.

'Malcolm!' My exclamation of surprise was

genuine. He was the last person I expected to see on my doormat.

'Can I come in?' He looked suspiciously at Billy as if expecting the little dog to bite his ankles.

'Of course — come in.' I stepped back from the door.

'I hoped I might catch you. I thought you might be having the rest of the day off after the funeral but I went to the bookshop just in case.'

'And Tom told you I was home? I didn't think he intended to open the shop today.'

'He didn't; the shop was closed. There was a notice on the door: *Closed due to family bereavement.*'

I murmured vaguely, 'Funerals take it out of you. Especially . . . ' My voice trailed away.

'Yes, I should imagine you are glad it is all over. I'm really sorry I had to rush off but I thought you bore up very well . . . considering.'

'Considering what? That I am the chief suspect — the last person to see poor Grace alive?' I was appalled to hear my voice rising to a shrill quaver with more than a hint of hysteria in it.

'No, of course I wasn't going to say that.' Malcolm began, but stopped when I shocked us both by bursting into tears.

He put his arm round me and I leaned against him. 'Come on,' he urged, 'come and sit down and I'll make you a nice cup of tea.'

'No! I'm awash with tea — and coffee.' I choked back a hysterical giggle, 'I'm sorry to be so silly — it's just that — '

'You are stressed out with it all and I don't wonder. Come and sit down anyway and I'll fix you something stronger.'

My legs felt strangely rubbery as he led me to the couch. He sat down beside me as I dropped down on it thankfully. 'There . . . ' He felt in his pocket and produced a large white hanky. He didn't pass it to me but gently mopped up my tears. I gulped noisily in my attempt to stop the absurd flow.

'You are behaving like one of Grace's heroes,' I told him. 'Or at least like the one in there.' I pointed to the pile of papers.

'Is that her latest book?' He followed my glance. 'The unfinished one?' He sounded totally uninterested and went on to ask, 'Now, what have you got to drink — other than tea or coffee?'

It was much, much later that I asked myself how Malcolm knew that Grace had left an unfinished book.

Now, I sniffed. 'I've got brandy — left over from last Christmas.'

He found the bottle, examined the label

with a slight downturn of his lips, then probed my cabinet for a glass. The measure he poured was generous, as befitted the tumbler he was pouring it into. I thought that it was far more likely to knock me out than revive me but I raised it to my lips and gasped as the fiery liquid hit my throat.

'Thank you, you are very kind,' I managed after a few breathless moments.

'Not really, just practical. I want to talk to you and you were hardly in a fit state to talk sensibly.'

'And you think I am now?' I nodded ironically at the glass.

'I thought it better not to intrude on the family after the funeral.' The self-effacing considerateness of his voice did not ring true.

'But Malcolm, there is no family. Grace didn't have anyone other than me — at least that is what I thought until the police said some . . . stepson had identified her.'

'What stepson?'

The brandy was making me belligerent, and this conversation was going over old ground. 'Grace did not have a stepson. We've been over all that.'

'I don't think the police could make a mistake like that.'

'If she did, and if he really was the person who identified the — identified Grace, then where is he now?' I was defensive; Malcolm's insistence that if the police said Grace had a stepson, then she did, annoyed me. 'He wasn't at the funeral as far as I know and no one seems to know where he is. Not even the solicitors. Surely he would come forward — if he exists — I mean, he might inherit some or all of her estate?'

'Not necessarily. She may have left a will leaving it elsewhere — to you perhaps. Have you thought of that?'

'Well, it crossed my mind,' I admitted, 'but I dismissed the thought. It didn't seem, well — it didn't seem quite nice when she was only just dead. Besides, Josh Smethurst just said I was to have this packet of papers; she left instructions it was to be given to me when she died.'

'These, you mean?' Malcolm indicated the untidy heap of papers. 'What is it?' He picked up a few pages, glanced through them and tossed them back again, 'Looks like the typescript of a book.'

'That is exactly what it is. Apparently Grace wrote romantic novels under a pen-name, this is her last, her work in progress; she bequeathed it to me. To tell you the honest truth I am not terribly impressed; I can't imagine her writing it. It doesn't seem to be Grace.' I don't know why but I didn't mention that she had also left me the rights in all her other, published, books.

He shrugged. 'Look, sweetie, I can see you are uptight and frazzled at the moment. What you need is a good rest. Why don't you go and lie down for an hour or so and I'll be back later and we'll go out to dinner?'

'Umm,' I murmured. True I felt confused and exhausted and didn't honestly think the brandy had helped. But Malcolm was being very kind and it was a good suggestion. 'I think I'll do that.'

'I'll be back around seven,' he told me as he got to his feet.

I went towards the bedroom, then turned back to call Billy. Malcolm was bent over the table, apparently reading one of the sheets of paper. He straightened up quickly when he realized I was watching him. 'I was just tidying these a bit for you.'

I went into my bedroom followed by Billy and flopped down on the bed. I was utterly spent.

Maybe the brandy had helped after all was my last conscious thought as I drifted off.

I woke an hour or so later shaking my head as I tried physically to free myself of a bewildering dream. It was all about that wretched typescript; even in sleep I failed to rid myself of it: Grace's latest book, if that was what it really was, and Billy, who was wading earnestly through the papers with a pair of horn-rimmed spectacles on his nose, as if searching for something. I began to laugh; at least this was amusing; then I stopped and began to think. Was there a message here? Was someone trying to get some information over to me, and if so, what and who? Grace immediately came to mind, to be followed almost as quickly by questions about my own sanity. The idea that my worldly-wise and intelligent aunt was attempting to contact me through my dreams was as absurd as the dream itself; wasn't it?

It did seem odd, though, that in some way or other everyone I knew who had known Grace showed interest in that wretched typescript. The only one who hadn't was Billy, now even he, in my dreams at any rate, was showing curiosity about it. Was I missing some piece of vital information?

As I padded across to pick up the wad of papers I toyed with the idea of another drink, hair of the dog, but decided against it. I didn't need anything that would dull my wits. I dropped down into my most comfortable chair and began to read. I was several pages in when I began to see it differently. What I had thought was poor fiction, not worthy of Grace, began to read differently and the astonishing idea crossed my mind that it was not actually fiction at all but non-fiction and that if Grace were the writer then it was probably her own story. What I had thought was just another novel was in fact her autobiography.

14

My interest was sharpened by the idea. I read
eagerly and was soon engrossed. The central
theme was still a love story, but reading it as
Grace's own personal history gave the
characters and events new meaning. I chided
myself for not realizing at once just what it
was but excused myself because it was written
in the third person. Had my aunt chosen to
write it in the first person it would probably
have been immediately obvious.

Grace had called her main character Faith
and that, I realized, was a clue in itself. I read
swiftly through the early part which dealt
mainly with Faith, or Grace's, life in England.
I concentrated on every word and every
nuance of meaning when I reached the part
where she left for Australia. I felt convinced
that the key to all the mystery surrounding
my aunt's death was hidden somewhere in
this part of the novel, or autobiography. The
fact that Grace had never mentioned living in
Australia to me, convinced me that it was a
significant phase of her life.

People either talked a lot about something
that was very important to them or didn't

mention it at all. Usually the latter if they did not have good memories of that time in their life. The fact that Grace had never mentioned Australia suggested to me that it was a period which she would prefer to forget. Even that there was something hidden in this part of her life that she preferred to remain hidden — a stepson, for instance?

The more I read the more I could see likenesses and parallels between the Grace I had known and the Faith of the book. I was so absorbed in the story that the realization that it had suddenly ceased to make sense brought me up short with a sharp pang of irritation and disappointment. I reread the last paragraph and turned back to the previous page before checking the page numbers. I rechecked, rubbing the sheets between finger and thumb; perhaps they had somehow got stuck together. No, two pages were missing unless they had somehow got into another part of the manuscript. It could have happened quite easily when they all fell to the floor and I collected them up in a hurry. Carefully and systematically I went through the pile of typescript. The pages did not appear to be there, so I started again at the beginning and still failed to find them. Feeling angry and frustrated I dropped to my knees to search beneath the furniture, it was just possible they could have slid out of sight. I was doing this when a car pulled up outside. Damn, I thought, it must be Malcolm; engrossed in my reading I had entirely forgotten he was coming back to take me out to dinner.

I bundled the remaining papers together and started shoving them into their envelope reflecting wryly that if Grace's writing could make me lose track of time so completely it must have some merit. I was surprised to open the door to see Malcolm's back; he was staring at the next-door flat — where Derek lived.

When he turned round to face me I could see that he was annoyed, even upset about something, but when his scowl was so quickly replaced by a smile I thought I was imagining things.

'Oh, Malcolm, I'm so sorry: I'm not ready.' My guilty apology was genuine enough but I didn't offer an explanation beyond. 'I didn't realize the time. I won't be a second.' I turned back into the house, anxious to scoop up the manuscript on the coffee table. It was all too obvious that I had been reading it. I didn't ask myself why I minded Malcolm knowing that. Anyway he guessed instantly.

'Were you reading that bundle of papers your aunt left you — some sort of manuscript, I believe?'

I nodded vaguely as I gathered up the remaining scattered sheets, trying to remember what I had told him about them.

'It must be engrossing if you forgot I was coming to take you out,' he remarked rather peevishly.

'Not really.' I shrugged, irritated by his tone. 'It just seems to be another of my aunt's books; she wrote romantic novels but this hardly seems up to the standard of those already published. Make yourself comfortable,' I told him as I put the untidy bundle on the table. 'I will be as quick as I can.'

When I returned to the lounge after the quickest tart-up of my life, Malcolm was at the window staring at my neighbour's flat in much the same way as I had found him when I opened the door.

'What do you find so absorbing in the place next door?' I tried to keep the irritation out of my voice. I had fallen over myself to get ready quickly and he was not even looking impatient.

Malcolm didn't answer immediately and I wondered if he had even heard me.

'Nothing,' he said as he turned to face me. 'Nothing at all; but I am interested in the occupant and why he has chosen to live there.'

'Probably because it happened to be available when he was looking for somewhere to live.' I picked up my handbag from the bench and added, when he continued staring through the window, 'I'm ready, Malcolm.'

I was halfway out through the door when he said, 'What about the dog?'

'What about him?' I heard the defensive note in my voice and told myself I sounded like an over-anxious, over-protective parent.

'Aren't you going to put him out?'

'Of course not.'

'Well, where is he?'

I glared at Malcolm for a moment before admitting, 'I left him in my bedroom.'

I walked out through the door hoping my action would convey that that was exactly where I meant him to be. I deduced from Malcolm's expression that he would have liked to haul poor Billy outside but he contented himself by muttering under his breath something about *Mummy's spoiled darling* and pulled the door closed unnecessarily hard as he joined me on the path.

I bit my lip as I slid into the passenger seat. I was at a bit of a loss myself to understand my own feelings about the little dog. I had taken him into my care as much as a favour that needed to be discharged towards Grace as for the dog's sake. What seemed to me

Malcolm's totally unreasonable reaction to him made me angry and more protective. Although I had known Billy as a sort of appendage to Grace, it was only since he had come to live with me that I had learned to know him as a personality in his own right and to appreciate his companionship.

'I've booked a table at the Golden Pheasant.' Malcolm's voice broke into my thoughts.

'Oh.' I wished he hadn't chosen the restaurant where Grace and I had dined on that last fateful evening of her life.

'It is by far the best place in town,' Malcolm pointed out, noting my lack of enthusiasm. 'In fact it is about the only really decent place. But if you would rather go somewhere else . . . ?'

'No, the Golden Pheasant is fine,' I agreed listlessly; after all I couldn't spend the rest of my life avoiding places in such a small town. 'Bentleigh isn't such a bad place, you make it sound . . . ' My voice trailed away as I tried to find the right word.

'A one-horse dump?'

I let my glance flick sideways; in the light of the street-lamps I could see a smile touching his lips. 'Is that what you were going to say?'

I nodded. 'Well — not exactly. I couldn't think of the right expression.'

'Well, if I made it sound like that then I was probably right.'

'Of course you weren't. It is a very pleasant town, just the right size, small enough to be personal, large enough to have everything one needs.'

'Like the Golden Pheasant?' From his voice I was not sure whether Malcolm was teasing or if he really felt that way.

All the same I felt my heart constrict as I walked through the main doors ahead of him. I wished we were somewhere else, the pain and grief that I had kept more or less beneath the surface threatened to overcome me as I recalled the happy evening I had spent the day before my birthday with Grace. I gulped and blinked my eyes hard.

I squared my shoulders and tried not to imagine that everyone in the reception area was looking at me, not just the hotel staff but other guests. I could guess their thoughts, even if I could not actually hear them muttering to one another: *That's the niece of that woman who was murdered; she was having dinner with her the night she was killed — yes, here. Last person to see her alive . . .* And so on. Just when I was afraid I might freak out and bolt for the exit I heard my aunt's voice in my head, or thought I did, saying, just as I had heard her so many times,

165

Most people are far too busy thinking about themselves to give anyone else a thought — so stop worrying. I smiled at the receptionist, tilted my chin and walked briskly into the dining room.

I really could not complain about Malcolm, he was attentiveness itself, the trouble was I simply could not forget the last time I had eaten there. Memories of Grace were so strong that at times it almost felt as if she was here in reality. I smiled absently at the waiter as he handed each of us a menu, ran my eyes down the printed words, but the only thing that stood out was what I had eaten with Grace: salmon. I sighed. 'Oh, I don't know what to have.' I looked over my menu at Malcolm, who was studying his with a slight frown. 'You choose,' I told him, 'Anything but the salmon.'

'I thought you liked — '

'I do — I just don't feel like it tonight.'

'Are you all right? You look a bit . . . wan.'

I glared at him across the table. That, I thought was all I wanted to hear. 'I'm fine — just fine.' I told him briskly. Adding under my breath: *considering . . .*

I made a supreme effort to be a pleasant companion for the rest of the evening. Malcolm, it seemed, was doing the same thing, but it made for a strained, not a relaxed, atmosphere between us. He appeared to be as relieved as I was when he delivered me back home.

'Will you come in for a drink — coffee, or something?' I offered insincerely.

'Not tonight — thanks all the same. I can see you are tired. I'll be in touch,' he answered, then startled me before I could get out of the passenger seat by leaning across, one arm in front of me to prevent my reaching the door handle. I turned in his arms, my protest killed on my lips as his mouth came down on mine with a harshness I found repelling.

'You *are* tired — I'm sorry.' His voice was gruff as he dropped his arms and released the catch on the door. I stepped out of the car, wondering if I might have reacted differently had I not been taken by surprise.

'Goodnight, Malcolm. Thank you for a lovely evening,' I heard myself say in a voice reminiscent of my six-year-old self after a party I had not really enjoyed. Because I felt vaguely guilty I might have returned his kiss, maybe a light touch on his cheek, but he had turned away and was once more giving his attention to the flat where Derek lived. So I stepped out of the car and turned my back, fumbled for my key and let myself in.

After closing the doors behind me I leaned

against it. Malcolm was right. I was more than tired; I was totally wiped out. I switched the lights on and looked round, the flat was quiet — too quiet. I had become used to the sound of claws clicking across the floor accompanied by the funny snuffling that was Billy's way of greeting me. He must be asleep in the bedroom. I switched on more lights. There was no sign of him. A quick search of the small apartment and anxious calls of 'Billy — Billy — where are you?' produced nothing — only a silence that convinced me he was not there.

Panic, laced with guilt, assailed me. Could I possibly have let him out accidentally when I went with Malcolm? Snatching up a torch I rushed outside and shone it round the tiny patio garden. There was no sign of him. There was a light in Derek's place, so I raced round and hammered on the door. I almost fell inside when it opened suddenly and Derek faced me. Absurdly, I burst into tears of sheer relief. Billy was in his arms.

15

My relief at seeing the little dog safe back-flipped to fury. What on earth was this — this — man doing with him? To my embarrassment, the tears, of rage now, spilled from my eyes and rained down my cheeks. My fury, originally directed at Derek, turned inward. How could I make such an idiot of myself?

I tried to take a deep breath. It ended in a huge gulp and I tried unsuccessfully to force myself to speak calmly. 'Give him to me,' I snapped tersely, adding somewhat belatedly, 'please.'

He made no move to hand the dog over, and Billy, damn the little traitor, made no attempt to get out of his arms. Quite the opposite; he gazed up at Derek with canine adoration and a long pink tongue reached out and slurped up his rescuer's face. Or it would have done if Derek, seeing it coming, had not leaned back so that it missed him by a whisker. Billy, I thought, gave a whole new dimension to the expression 'air kissing'. Even if he failed to make a physical connection Billy certainly made it obvious that he considered his rescuer a pretty nice guy.

'I don't think you should leave him outside when you go out with your boyfriend.' Derek made no move to hand him over.

My jaw dropped at the gross injustice of the remark.

'I didn't leave him outside.' As I spoke the words I knew with absolute certainty that I was speaking the truth. 'I left him asleep, well, dozing anyway, in his basket in my bedroom,' I told him through gritted teeth. I was about to add that I remembered perfectly because Malcolm had objected but decided to leave that bit unsaid and muttered, 'Malcolm is not my boyfriend. I can assure you I left the wretched little dog inside, locked inside. So tell me: what is he doing here with you?'

Billy turned sad brown eyes on me and I immediately felt guilty for calling him a wretched little dog. I was on the point of apologizing to him when Derek, thrusting him in my direction, almost shouted, 'I did not break in and dognap him if that is what you are suggesting. I heard a noise, from the direction of your flat. When I looked out of my bathroom window I could see the garbage bin had been knocked over. I thought the wind or a marauding cat was responsible and

— like the good neighbour I am, thought I should pick up the rubbish and put it back. As I opened my door I caught a glimpse of someone leaving, very hurriedly, through your gate. I had seen you go out earlier so I knew it wasn't you.'

I snorted, indignant at the thought that he had been keeping track of my comings and goings. Derek ignored me. 'Whoever they were they were in too big a hurry to shut the gate. I went to pick up your rubbish, intending to close it when I left. That was when I saw Billy was outside so I grabbed him before he went out on the road. I couldn't put him back indoors because I have no key. I thought of just leaving him where he was, then I thought someone else might come along and leave the gate open so I brought him round here, intending to hand him over as soon as I heard you come back. I thought I would hear you get home and bring him straight round before you got worried. I didn't hear you — sorry about that — so I kept him safe inside my flat. I assure you I had no ulterior motive.'

'Hmmph.' I was uncomfortably aware that I sounded both ungracious and ungrateful. In spite of that some inner demon made me say, 'How do I know you weren't the person who — who went in and stole him?'

Derek's mouth dropped open in astonishment at my attitude before tightening in a thin line. I could see him wondering if I had taken in a word he had said, or did I simply not believe he was speaking the truth?

'Because . . . ' He spoke very slowly, obviously trying hard to keep his temper, 'I don't have any possible reason to take your dog, but I do happen to like the little fellow and didn't want him to come to any harm.' He pointed to Billy as he spoke. 'Now look after him!' he added curtly, then he turned towards his own open door. Before he closed it he looked back to advise, 'I should change the locks on your door if I were you. I haven't got a key, but obviously someone has.'

I stared at the closed door, ashamed of my graceless behaviour. My mumbled apologies and thanks were lost on the night air. I clutched Billy close, more for my own comfort than his. As I reached my own door I realized that it was my own heart hammering, not, as I had first thought, Billy's heart thumping against my body that I could feel. The thought that some person unknown possessed a key to my door was very scary.

If only I could replay my conversation with Derek. It would have been a comfort to have someone, other than Billy, although he was certainly better than nothing, to go through that door with me. As I fumbled with the door he began to tremble, no doubt catching my own fears. For the second time that night I fumbled with the lock; this time my fingers shook so much I had real difficulty getting the key in place. I would have swallowed my pride and run back next door, but I had heard the door slam shut. Taking a deep breath and making a supreme effort to control the shake in my fingers I worked the key into the lock and let myself in. I switched on any lights not already on and made a thorough and systematic search of every room, checking that windows were closed and latched as I did so. Last of all I went into the bedroom where Billy was already ensconced on my bed. I experienced a sliver of comfort when I felt his small body against my thigh as I crept into bed.

Haunted by the thought that some person I did not know, or — and this was even more scary — I did, could come and go in my home was totally unnerving. A quick tour of the flat had convinced me that nothing had been taken. This was not a comfort; if burglary was not their motive then what was? The fear that prickled up my spine was more than a slight *frisson*; it was enough to make me lie sleepless and rigid, straining my ears for any untoward sound, and I kept several lights on. I was glad Derek had kept Billy safe even though his absence had scared me at first.

I jumped so hard when my phone rang that I almost knocked poor Billy off the bed. Afraid of what I might hear I decided not to answer it, but it had barely stopped when my mobile rang. Visualizing an entire night sitting up in bed listening to phones that I was too jittery to answer, I said, 'Yes?' in a wobbly and slightly squeaky voice that sharpened with relief at the familiar voice. 'Malcolm, what on earth are you ringing me for?'

'Just to make sure you are all right. I thought you seemed rather frazzled when I left you.'

'I'm fine — absolutely fine.' To my dismay the wobble was back in my voice.

'You don't sound fine to me.' He sounded dubious and I was touched by what I thought was concern in his voice.

'Well, to tell you the truth I'm a bit scared,' I admitted. *A bit scared* — what did I mean? Scared witless was more like it. 'Someone broke in while I was out with you.'

'Good God, why didn't you call me? I feel dreadful. I should never have let you go in by yourself. Did they take anything — do much damage?'

I shook my head forgetting he couldn't see

me, then mumbled, 'I don't think so.' My voice quavered as it crossed my mind that in an odd way that made it scarier; what were they looking for and if they hadn't found it did that mean they would be back?

'Hang on. I'll be there just as soon as I can. Don't answer the door to anyone but me.'

'There's no need . . . ' I began, then realized that I was talking to a dead phone. I sighed, debating whether to get dressed again or just put on my dressing-gown. I opted for the latter and, instructing Billy to stay where he was, I went into the kitchen and switched on the electric kettle.

It was just coming to the boil when I heard a car door slam outside. Squinting through the window I saw Malcolm walking up to my door. As I let him in I wondered how he had managed to get here so quickly.

'I was just making tea,' I told him. 'Would you like a cup — or coffee?'

'You look as if you need something stronger. Tea may be your standard remedy for everything but you must be awash with it by now.' Without more ado or a by-your-leave he opened the cupboard where he knew I kept any drink I had and peered inside. 'Whisky!' he exclaimed, managing to sound shocked, surprised and pleased all at once. 'That's more like it!'

'Not for me,' I told him firmly. 'I'll stick to tea if you don't mind.' I felt annoyed at the way he was taking over. 'You have what you like, just don't expect me to drink it, I hate the stuff.' This was true, but I also had the feeling that I needed to keep my wits functioning.

He shrugged, then poured himself what, to me, seemed a very large slug. I dropped a teabag into the pot then turned to the fridge for the milk. I glanced back just in time to see him transfer a substantial splash from his glass into my mug.

'You need it — medicinal purposes.'

16

I supposed Malcolm thought he was being kind but anguish and annoyance were the only feelings that surged up within me. I had meant it when I said I didn't want whisky. It was one drink I loathed. I had entirely forgotten about that bottle lurking in the back of my drinks cupboard and Malcolm's reminder that it was there was also a sharp reminder that Grace was dead. The bottle had been bought specifically for Grace. It was what she drank as a nightcap at home — purely for medicinal purposes, she always claimed with a twinkle — and what she liked to have in her hand to sip slowly and appreciatively when visiting. I usually drank a glass of wine and both of us made one glass do for the evening when we were visiting each other and had settled for a relaxing chat. Even though I knew that would never happen again I burned with anger and resentment as I watched Malcolm raise the generous drink, scarcely diluted by the splash of water he had added to it. That whisky was for Grace and no one else had any right to it.

Turning my back on him I managed to

dispose of my own drink down the sink and quickly poured myself another cup, free of the noxious liquid. I was surprised he made no comment, then I saw, to my surprise, that he was leafing through the pages of Grace's book. This was cause for more irritation on my part. He had made concern for me the excuse to invade my privacy and get me out of bed, but all he was doing was making himself free with my whisky and my possessions.

He looked up suddenly, as if aware of my scrutiny. 'Come and sit down,' he invited. 'Are you enjoying your tea?'

'Very much, thanks!' I smiled inwardly; he couldn't have noticed that I had disposed of his 'doctored' drink and that I was actually sipping, slowly, hoping he wouldn't guess what I had done, at nothing stronger than a good cup of tea.

Malcolm tapped the pile of papers with one forefinger. 'Did your aunt make any money out of this sort of thing?' My heightened sensibilities flinched at the note of disbelieving derision that I detected in his voice.

'Her books, I believe, were — are — very popular.'

'Oh well, there is no accounting for tastes. Personally I couldn't read the stuff.'

Since that was exactly what he had given

every appearance of doing a few minutes earlier I could not resist saying tartly, 'How lucky you don't have to, then.' He didn't respond, which I suppose was a good thing; the last thing I needed was involvement in an argument at this time of night. I just wanted to return to bed. I sighed and yawned ostentatiously, hoping to get this message across. Apparently I succeeded as Malcolm dropped the manuscript disdainfully back on to the coffee table and turned towards me.

'You look a bit pale. If you are sure you will be all right I might as well go.'

'I feel more than a bit pale, I feel absolutely washed out,' I retorted, adding another yawn for good measure. 'It was . . . kind of you to call and see if I am all right. Well, now you can see that I am I would like to go back to bed.'

'Trot off then, don't let me stop you.'

'But you are stopping me. I need to lock the door after you.'

'I can lock it as I go.'

'There is a chain inside,' I pointed out. 'You can't do that from outside and I would feel much safer if I knew it was done.'

I had snibbed the lock, listened with relief to Malcolm's car starting up and was fastening the chain when I realized that had this been done earlier no one could have got in and Billy could not have got out. I was climbing into bed before I remembered pointing out to Malcolm that one had to be inside the house to do that. Which, of course, meant that it would have been impossible for me to do it. Telling myself my mind was slipping, I crawled into bed. Billy wagged his tail then settled down against my feet. I considered ordering him into his own bed, but it was comforting to feel him so close. I dropped off to sleep considering that Billy had remained in the bedroom with Malcolm in the house. I was sure that if my visitor had been Derek, Billy would have been at the door at the double to greet him. Pondering hazily on the significance of this and sure there was some, I fell asleep.

* * *

On the Sunday morning I woke with mixed feelings: relief that it was Sunday and I did not have to go to work, and the ever-present grief each time I remembered what had happened to Grace. Billy was eager to be up and about so I slipped into a robe and let him out into my tiny patio garden before switching on the kettle for the invariable coffee to kick-start my day. As I waited for it to brew and the toast to pop up I mused over the events of the evening and the funeral. Malcolm's lack of interest was quite obviously feigned, or so it appeared to me now. Had I thought that at the time, or was it now only the wisdom of hindsight? I wasn't entirely sure but I was even more convinced that there was something of importance to be learned in the unpublished book left for me by Grace. I took my coffee and toast over to my comfortable recliner and riffled through the pages to find the spot where I had left off reading.

I soon came across it by checking the page numbers until I came to page 97; the next page was numbered 107. Nine pages either missing or out of sequence. Carefully I went through the sheets of typescript. The last page was number 225 so the missing bit was almost in the middle. I worked through them again, this time working backwards, then through the pages I had already read, just in case the missing bit could have got back there somehow and I had missed it. I read the last couple of lines on page 97 then looked at the top of page 107. As the last bit that I read ended in the middle of a sentence and the top of the next page began with a new paragraph it was obvious it did not follow on. However, I read the last lines of the page where the break began and the beginning of the next page: I had to make sure. It quite definitely did not make sense. As a thought worked through my mind like a worm, I went back to where I had stopped reading. I had stopped because two pages were missing; these had reappeared but the following nine pages had gone. Wondering if I really was going slightly deranged, I dropped to the floor and began to crawl round my small home looking beneath furniture — I was sure I must have simply dropped them. I was overcome with a sense of *déjà vu* combined with the knowledge that expecting to find them was a forlorn hope. Nine A4 sheets of paper were not likely to be lying on the floor unseen. I stood up and moved the cushions in a final attempt to locate them.

Seething with frustration and the effort of convincing myself I was not mad, I knew perfectly well that two pages had vanished and reappeared and now a further nine had gone, I was more convinced than ever that there was something I needed to know in the missing pages, and it was a knowledge that someone else was determined to hide or keep to themselves. I scanned through the page after the break, but it simply did not make sense; it was obvious the reader was supposed to have absorbed the missing information. I slapped the page I was reading down on the unread pile with an exclamation of disgust and decided to shower and dress. The relaxing and therapeutic power of warm water had helped me solve problems in the past, but this, I was afraid was beyond me. As I stepped under the showerhead and felt the first spray of water, cold because I was too preoccupied to wait for it to warm up, I remembered that I had left Billy outside and wondered why I was so convinced that the pages had gone missing while in my possession. Wasn't it possible that I had never had them?

Concerned about the little dog, and wondering why he hadn't barked to come in, I rubbed shampoo into my hair and rinsed it out again as quickly as possible, reflecting irritably that remembering him had robbed me of the therapeutic and relaxing powers of the shower. As for inspiration, well, I was no nearer an answer to my problem than before. Or was I? If the pages had not gone missing while in my possession then the other possibility was that someone had removed them in the solicitor's office where they were supposed to be in safe keeping. Could Josh Smethurst be responsible?

Hastily towelled and casually dressed in jeans and a light sweater, my hair still damp, I went to let Billy in. When I opened the door he bounded in, so closely followed by Derek that I had little hope of shutting the door in his face without closing the dog's tail in it.

'*Do* come in!' I forced my voice to sound sarcastic and cursed the sudden stab of pleasure I felt at his smiling face. The preposterous man was always on, or worse, over my doorstep.

'Ah, you are up! I wondered if you were, Billy has been sitting outside the door patiently waiting for you to open it.'

'You, too, I suppose,' I snarled, and wondered how what was meant to be a cutting remark came out sounding warm and welcoming.

'Yup.' He grinned, totally unabashed. 'And now we are both ready for breakfast.'

'Too bad — I've had mine.' I remembered the single cup of coffee and the one thin slice of toast and knew I could easily forget that and start again.

As if he had read my thoughts Derek glanced at the coffee plunger still half-full of cooling coffee.

'Well.' I admitted that I had only had one cup of coffee and a bit of toast. I could drink another cup. I reached for a small saucepan, poured the almost cold coffee in it and put it on the gas to warm up while I added fresh grounds to the plunger and waited for the kettle to boil. I turned to see Derek smiling approvingly.

184

'Good girl. I would hate to see good coffee poured away just because it is cold.'

'You won't get any — cold or hot — if you call me 'good girl' again.'

'Billy doesn't mind me calling him 'good boy'.'

'Billy is a dog — I'm not!' I sounded huffy, but in spite of myself my lips twitched as I turned and saw the laughter in his eyes. 'Oh, go on with you. Do you want some toast too?'

★　★　★

'Penny for them?' Derek asked between sips of hot coffee. 'What's the problem? I can see something is worrying you.'

'Just about everything is,' I admitted with a heavy sigh. 'As if being broken into isn't enough, and me thinking Billy had been kidnapped, there are some pages missing in that wretched book that Grace left in manuscript form. I have this feeling that it has to be important and I have been reading it, then nearly halfway through there is a gap: nine pages missing. I have searched everywhere for them.'

'I thought you said the book wasn't much good.'

'I didn't say that. I said it was different — not like her others. It — well, it sort of rings true somehow. I can't explain it — I just feel those damn missing pages are the key to everything — if I could find those I would know why I'm being broken into — what it is that whoever it is wants.'

'Have you looked through Grace's flat?'

'Her flat — no.' I gave an involuntary shudder. 'To tell you the truth I haven't been there since I went there with the police immediately after she died.'

'Perhaps you should,' Derek said quietly, 'and for the record I did not kidnap Billy, I rescued him.'

I smiled. 'I know.' I looked at him, wondering if I could trust him, wondering, as I had before, just whom I could trust. 'Would — would you . . . ?'

'Will I come with you to Grace's flat; is that what you were going to ask? Of course I will if you really want me to. I suppose it is OK?'

'It should be. She left it to me, so I am told. The flat and the contents. I already have a key. Grace gave me one ages ago in case — in case anything happened to her and I needed it . . . ' My voice trailed away as I thought that my having a key had not helped much when something did happen.

17

I stabbed the key at the lock on Grace's door but the tears I was fighting to hold back blurred my vision so much that after three unsuccessful attempts Derek took the key gently from my trembling fingers and unlocked the door himself. He stood back to let me go in, but I shook my head; following him was easier than being the first to step over the threshold.

It was all so much as I remembered it that I half-expected to see Grace there, busy in the kitchen, reading in the big armchair or working on her laptop computer. I even expected Billy to run to greet me. The silence was absolute.

I looked round — something was wrong. 'Someone has been in here.'

'Are you sure? How can you tell?' Derek asked. 'It all looks pretty tidy and untouched to me.'

'Oh, I don't mean someone has turned it over; whoever it was probably knew just what they were looking for.' My eyes darted round the room.

'Her laptop — it's gone!' I exclaimed. 'The

police told me that they had returned it after examining what was on it. Nothing, they said, of any interest.'

Derek followed my gaze to the small desk on the other side of the room. The top was bare. 'She always kept it on that desk. It was only moved if she needed to take it with her. That was the only time she ever put it in its case.' I walked over to the desk. 'The case was always here — just at the side of the desk.' I pointed to the place where Grace kept it and turned to him. It suddenly struck me that as the manuscript was the hard copy of something she had written on the computer then the original was probably still on her laptop. I voiced this thought aloud. 'Oh, why didn't I think of that before?'

Derek frowned, 'You are not the only one — *I* hadn't thought of that either. Just a minute . . . ' I could see he was grappling with another idea. 'That manuscript was given to you by the solicitor. If your aunt wanted you and you only to read it and went to the trouble of printing it out and putting it in an envelope which she then deposited with the solicitors, surely she would not have left a copy on her computer where anyone could read it?'

'That makes sense,' I conceded, 'but if it was so important then surely she would not have made the only copy a printout. After all, sheets of paper can so easily be destroyed or lost.'

'Or partially lost; stolen even, as you have discovered.'

I stared at him. 'You are right of course. We are looking for the wrong thing, searching for sheets of paper. She would have put it on a disk somewhere.'

'And that is what we have to look for. Whoever it is who is so anxious to read the whole book doesn't seem to have thought of that, although they had obviously guessed that there might be a copy of the whole thing on the computer.'

'You're right, but you have missed the point.'

Derek looked at me in surprise. 'I have?'

'Yes. It is not that *they* want to read the whole thing — they have obviously done that — they don't want *me* to read it.'

'Some information is hidden in that innocent-looking manuscript that someone doesn't want you to know.' Derek spoke slowly as he thought this over before adding, 'Perhaps doesn't want anyone to know.'

'But Grace did want me to know . . . ' I mused, silent for a moment or two before, with a burst of exasperation I cried, 'Why the hell couldn't she have just *told* me whatever it

189

was she wanted me to know?'

'It would certainly have made for a simpler and easier life all round,' Derek conceded with a wry smile. 'But since she didn't let's see if we can find anything more.'

'I wonder where she kept her disks; she must have kept copies of her novels somewhere.' As I spoke I pulled open a drawer in the desk. 'Oh gosh . . . ' I groaned, 'she kept them all right — there must be copies of everything she ever wrote here.' I began to look through them reading the labels. 'It looks as if she used three different names. She must have written under three different pseudonyms.' I wondered why she had done that and added, half to myself, 'Josh Smethurst only told me the one she left to me. There are no titles on these disks, just book one, two and three and so on and then a name.'

'What name did she write the one we are looking for under?'

I screwed up my face, trying to remember. 'I can't remember,' I finally admitted.

'That means you will probably have to bring each one up on the computer till you find the right one,' Derek pointed out.

'Thanks for telling me; I had already figured that out. Come on, help me gather them up. I couldn't do it here, nor even down in the shop.' I knew there was a large old computer down there, the one she kept her business records on. 'I already feel I am poking about in her belongings. I'll take them home and put them up on my own computer.'

'Your belongings now, surely?' Derek pointed out, as he helped me put all the disks in a carrier bag.

'Thanks. You — you've been very helpful,' I told him when we reached my flat. He had been, and I felt guilty as I stood in front of my door willing him to go home. I wanted to be alone when I worked through Grace's disks and found out whatever there was to be found out. I liked Derek, even trusted him, or almost, and yet — after the events of the last week I felt there was no one I could really rely on. Malcolm's behaviour had been so odd since Grace died that I could hardly believe I had actually toyed with the notion of a serious relationship with him. I reminded myself that when I heard about my aunt's murder it had been Malcolm I had relied on for support and Derek who seemed so abrasive. Now the tables appeared to have turned. If only Grace were here: she had always had such a common-sense way of looking at things. I realized I was feeling the lack of a close female relative or friend to confide in, but in the time I had been living in the area I had not made many friends, had never been very outgoing and more often than not had been satisfied with my own company. The one close friend of my childhood, Tracey Bingham, had married and shortly afterwards gone with her husband to America.

Quashing my guilty feelings about not asking Derek in I closed the door firmly and carried the pile of disks through to my computer, which I fired up immediately. Aeons later, or so it seemed, I had worked through them all and not found the material I was looking for. I could have screamed with frustration. I simply could not believe that Grace would have left only the one copy of something she appeared to consider so important. Sheets of paper were so easy to destroy or lose. I slumped down in a chair and reached for the pile of typescript. In my frustration at discovering pages missing I had stopped reading. Perhaps that was stupid: I might learn something in the remaining pages. I began to read from the point after the break.

I was immediately pitchforked across the world. Grace certainly wrote of Australia as if she knew it well. I was even more convinced that this was autobiography, not fiction.

'Australia proved somewhat of a great culture shock.' I read, 'but one she quickly adapted to. The climate was easy enough; she had always enjoyed hot weather; but the vast distances and the lack of history and, she thought, lack of culture were something else. She was conceited and confident enough to feel that in coming out here as a governess she would be able to do something about the last of these. But, of course, her ignorance and naïvety was no match for the outback. When she had been interviewed in London and agreed to go out to Australia to take up a position as a governess she visualized an English farm dumped down in Australia with a little bit more sunshine thrown in and, of course, an Australian version of an English market town not too far away. Wellsford Downs measured itself in square miles — not acres — and the only way to get to it was by light plane. None of this Faith knew when she presented herself to the elder Mrs Wellsford in London. The older woman did not enlighten her, merely outlined the duties expected of her in caring for two young children. Probably, Faith thought after she had been at the station a few weeks, Mrs Wellsford had thought the less Faith knew the more likely she would be to accept the

*post. Recruiting governesses had proved
difficult enough in the past, as had keeping
them. Get the girl there and her job would
be over; it would be up to her son and
daughter-in-law to see she stayed. Blissful
in her ignorance and excited at the
prospect of adventure Faith set out for
Australia.'*

What I had just read whetted my appetite for
more. How strange, I thought. In all the years
I had known her Grace had never mentioned
this Antipodean episode in her life. Feeling
faintly hurt and excluded I returned to the
manuscript. What I read next added annoyance to those feelings.

Would I, Grace mused (the paragraph
inserted here changed to the first person,
leaving no doubt whose thoughts these were),
*have gone at all if I had guessed the half of
what lay before me? My time in Australia was
to turn out much more than a mere
adventure; it would change my whole life.* At
this point I felt like throwing the whole thing
out of the window. Reading this was proving a
futile exercise in frustration.

Nevertheless I read on, searching for some
explanation.

The next bit was interesting in an
anecdotal and historic way, but curiously

devoid of emotion. Grace wrote about the voyage out, of instructions to take a north-westbound train into the great outback to a town whose name, for some reason, had been blacked out. There Faith was met and taken the last leg of her long journey to Wellsford Downs. Scribbled into the typescript, in Grace's familiar handwriting, were the words: *This was the point where I began to doubt the wisdom of my 'great adventure'. This last stage of the journey was made in a truck whose bone-shaking progress was so noisy that conversation was almost impossible,* Grace, writing as Faith, recorded. *The heat was stifling and once they were clear of the little town the bitumen gave up and the unsealed road threw up clouds of red dust that rose around them like fog and even penetrated the interior of the cab.* Another insert in Grace's writing read: *'I thought I had arrived in Hell.'*

18

I read on doggedly till I reached the last page. It was, I decided, a singularly dull and rather depressing story.

When they arrived at the homestead, a large weatherboard house with a veranda running all round it, standing squarely in the centre of a cluster of farm sheds, cattle yards, sheep yards, chook yards, horse yards and a row of kennels housing chained dogs, the taciturn driver instructed Faith to follow as he humped her cases towards the veranda. Grace wrote. She found the house curiously quiet but assumed that the inhabitants were all about their own business somewhere. By the time she had unpacked in the bedroom where her cases had been dumped Faith was getting both curious and anxious and set out on a voyage of discovery. Following the sound of distant voices she discovered a large kitchen where two black women were preparing food. Playing on the floor was a small child, about two or three years old; this, she supposed, was one of her new charges. In fact he was the only one; young Mrs Wellsford had left a week before, ostensibly on holiday, taking her six-year-old daughter with her.

I waded through tedious pages of description about Grace's daily life. It was so dull that I could not believe my aunt could possibly have written this with a view to publication. When I reached the last page and the information, baldly stated, that the mistress of the house and her young daughter were not returning, I once more felt like hurling the whole story away in disgust. I wondered when Grace had written this dull and depressing piece of fiction or autobiography. And why on earth had she gone to the trouble of leaving it in a sealed envelope with her solicitors, to be handed to me after her death? Nothing about it made sense, least of all that anyone should imagine there was anything in this dreary piece of unpublished writing to make it worth stealing. I was sure now this was not fiction and if it was fact what had happened next? Had Faith, whom I was beginning to think of as Grace, stayed on in what she obviously considered exile, or had she returned to England? If this was Grace's own story, when had it taken place? In spite of myself I found I wanted to know more;

most of all, I needed to know how much of this story was true. I made up my mind to question Tom next day. He had known Grace for many years; if anyone knew about this period in her life it was probably him.

* * *

'Did Grace really go to Australia?' I tried to sound casual, as Tom and I enjoyed a coffee during a lull in the morning's business.

'I believe so.' The vague answer was not encouraging.

'How long did she stay there and what did she go for?'

'I couldn't say — it was before I knew her.' Tom stopped abruptly, looking faintly shocked, and I had the feeling that he had been about to add *You will have to ask her* before memory clicked in. After a moment's silence he added, 'She never talked about it. I got the impression it was a period in her life she would rather forget.' He got up and took his cup to the sink, making it clear that he did not intend to discuss Grace, and particularly Grace in Australia, any more. That much was evident from his posture as he returned to the shop.

'Well, she didn't forget,' I muttered to his retreating back before rinsing the mugs and following. Grace, I was sure, had never forgotten her time in Australia and for some reason she wanted me to know about it. What that reason was I couldn't fathom at the moment. I wondered why Tom had been so cagey when I questioned him; he had been curt almost to the point of rudeness. This was so unlike his normal polite vagueness that it convinced me that he knew a lot more than he was prepared to admit. Perhaps he was chivalrously protecting some dark secret in my aunt's life. I was momentarily carried away by romantic ideas that I knew were absurd. Grace had always been such a straight down the line sort of person for that to be possible.

'Do you mind if I borrow one of Grace's novels?' I asked, as I tidied the shelf where they lived. My eye had been caught by a gap in the line of books, causing one to lean over. Frowning slightly I righted it and slid along other books to fill in the gap. I supposed someone must have bought one or more. Tom must have served them; I would not have forgotten if a customer had purchased any while I was in the shop.

'You know you can borrow any book in the shop so long as you return it.' Tom still sounded testy, I thought. 'Death must be good publicity.' His tone was cynical. 'Those books have been there for ages and two people have come in and bought one this week, since Grace — er — died, and now you want to read one.'

I chose a book more or less at random; I just wanted to see if there was enough difference in style to confirm my hunch that the unpublished typescript Grace had left me was not fiction. 'I don't suppose you remember anything about the people who bought them, do you, Tom?'

I had asked the question casually, quite sure he would answer in the negative. His reply not only surprised me but also rang a vague warning in my head.

'I most certainly do. In fact I have been wondering whether I should mention it to you or not, as it struck me as odd . . . ' His words trailed off as he still seemed to be debating within himself whether or not to tell me.

'Who bought them, Tom?' I felt I needed to know.

'Well, the first odd thing was that they were bought by young men. Light romances are usually bought by women. The second strange coincidence was they both know you.'

My first reaction was that one of them must be that sticky beak of a reporter who had moved in next door. 'I suppose one of them was Derek — my neighbour?'

'Derek? Oh, no. It was that young solicitor who is handling your aunt's affairs. He tried to give me some garbled excuse about his secretary wanting to read one of her books. If that was so then why didn't she come in herself?'

'Oh!' I gave a small gasp of surprise; this was not what I had expected to hear at all. 'And the other — who was the other?'

'That fellow you've been going out with — Malcolm what's his name.' That was what I expected to hear; after all there were only three young men I knew in the district and if it wasn't Derek and one was Josh then there was no one else left but Malcolm. But why on earth could either of them possibly want to read my aunt's novels? Unless they too were searching for information. I needed to find out what it was, preferably before someone else did. 'Could I borrow all of them?' I asked. 'There are only five. I'll bring them back.'

'Of course you can — and as for bringing them back — keep them. I am sorry to have to say they don't really add to the prestige of the business.' He gave me a wry smile. I thanked him and privately agreed. Tom had built up his shop and his reputation on good-quality books, mostly out of print, and antiquarian books. I wondered why he had my aunt's books on the shelves in the first place. Although he stocked children's fiction it was mostly the classics; modern romantic fiction did not really fit in at all.

'I suppose it was a sentimental whim that made me put them there.' Tom, answering the question that I had not spoken aloud, startled me and I looked across the shop in surprise. He was sitting staring into space with a look of almost unbearable sadness on his face. As I watched he appeared to pull himself together with a shrug that was both mental and physical. I decided to drop the subject of my aunt's writing and anything else about her.

It was a dank, cold day and dark by the time I got home. Typical December, I reflected gloomily, as I turned the key in my own lock. Billy would have to make do with the backyard; I had no intention of walking him today. Because I felt twinges of guilt about not walking him I didn't mind at all when the familiar red ball bounced on the ground in front of the little dog, I knew he would get both exercise and enjoyment chasing it round the tiny backyard, so I made no attempt to pick it up and throw it over the fence. I was about to go back inside when I heard a child's voice behind me. 'Can I have my ball back, please!'

Turning, I saw Jimmy's anxious face over

the top of the fence and felt bad that I had planned not to throw it back.

'Of course!' I assured him and turned to retrieve it from Billy, who was enjoying his solo game, pushing it round the yard at high speed with his nose, and not at all keen to give it up. Jimmy's excited laughter egged him on and the laughter became a shriek of joy when I, reaching desperately for the ball, skidded on damp slippery grass to land on my butt with an undignified thud. I looked up to see Jimmy's smiling face had been joined by that of his uncle a broad grin stretched from ear to ear on Derek's face.

'Oh — very funny!' I gritted as I scrambled to my feet.

Derek looked completely unabashed. 'Yes — it was.' He had the temerity to agree with me. 'You should use a bit of strategy.'

'Such as?' I fought to keep the humiliation and anger out of my voice.

'Distract the dog — then move in and get the ball yourself.'

'Yes, well . . . ' I had to admit the suggestion smacked of commonsense and looked round for something that would grab Billy's attention.

'Billy — here, Billy!' Derek called in a falsetto voice vibrating with the promise of excitement even greater than the ball. When the dog bounded over to the fence I seized the chance to pick the ball up and hurl it towards next door. I saw both heads duck as the red missile flew between them. The sight of Derek's head disappearing somewhat mitigated the humiliation of sitting down with such lack of dignity.

'Bad shot! You missed me!'

'I wasn't aiming at you,' I admitted truthfully, and turned to go back into my own flat. I was uncomfortably aware that my seat felt damp and was probably muddy; the small patch of grass where I had sat so unceremoniously was both.

'Angie, wait a minute!'

I turned reluctantly.

'It's nearly Christmas.'

'I know.' Of course I knew — and I was not looking forward to it. Grace's absence would be a painful reminder of happy childhood Christmases.

'What are you doing about it?'

'Tom is having lunch with me and — and I am going out in the evening.' A curious reluctance made me hesitate at this point. 'Why do you want to know?'

'I see.' Derek sounded disappointed. 'I just thought — well, I hoped that maybe we could join up with you. You see, Jimmy will be here with me; his mother has had to go into hospital and it doesn't look as if she will be out. Won't be much of a Christmas for a kid, just with me.'

I looked at the child staring at me anxiously. Billy was looking up at him. When Jimmy's glance fell on him he gave an excited yap and jumped on the ball as Jimmy dropped it over the fence. 'Sorry!' Jimmy sounded anything but and his grin confirmed it. The innocent pleasure of the child and the dog in each other's company touched me in spite of my irritation; they were just two lonely youngsters — I should show some Christmas spirit and make the most of it.

'Why don't you come round and join Tom and me?'

'That would be great — we would love to, wouldn't we, Jimmy?' The expression on the child's face gave his answer. 'While we are on the subject of Christmas, what about Christmas Eve? I know it is asking a huge favour of you, but I wonder if you could come round for a drink and a mince pie — or something. The truth is I need some help with a little job I have to do.' He tipped his head slightly towards Jimmy who was leaning over the fence loudly urging Billy on to greater exploits with the ball.

'Yes, of course,' I murmured. Put like that how could I refuse? I retrieved the ball from

Billy, this time without difficulty as he was getting slightly bored playing by himself, even with an enthusiastic audience. I tossed it carefully over the fence and, with a casual ''Bye for now!' turned to my own door. As I closed it behind me I wondered how I had got inveigled into spending most of Christmas with Derek. I wondered even more at how pleased I felt at the prospect.

19

When Malcolm first invited me to have dinner with him and his parents on Christmas night I had been elated. Meeting the parents had a ring of promise to it, even if it did seem a tad old-fashioned. I was still clinging then to the idea of a romantic relationship with Malcolm. Now I was pretty sure he had forgotten all about it, after all three months in advance is a long time to issue a dinner invitation, even for Christmas. I found myself wondering if there was any way I could slither gracefully out of the arrangement if he mentioned it again. I refused to connect Derek in any way with my change of heart.

Grace, I thought would have remarked tartly that men always complicated things; women could cope without them. She might have added one of her favourite aphorisms: *She travels furthest who travels alone.* But I had always envied my friends with two parents, siblings and a full home life. In my heart I knew that in many ways I had been lucky; when my parents died and Grace appeared and took me under her wing I had more of a home than when they were alive. I certainly never lacked for anything in my growing years. It seemed that the lesson and the legacy of my childhood had been a yearning for a home and children of my own. Apart from a few casual boyfriends and one disastrous relationship with a man who had backed off in terror when confronted with my ambition to be a wife and mother, only then revealing that he was already married with a family, Malcolm had been the first person who seemed to offer fulfilment for my dreams.

The three months since Grace died had been as grey and dreary as a perpetual November with, it seemed, little headway being made by the police in solving my aunt's murder, but now, with Christmas drawing nearer and the shops full of commercial good cheer I found my spirits lifting. Sorry as I was for Derek's sister spending Christmas in hospital I was glad to have a child to think about and to buy presents for.

I only wished I knew a bit more about small boys and the sort of things they liked. Big boys too, I reflected. I had Malcolm, Derek and, of course, Tom to think about if I would be spending time over the holiday with all of them. My mind being busy with planning for the coming festivities thoughts about Grace's books, even the one that was partly missing, took a back seat. I was unprepared for the phone call from Josh Smethurst.

'Miss Divine?' I permitted myself a small smile when I answered the phone and recognized the impeccable manners almost before I recognized the voice. 'I would very much appreciate it if you could call round at my office. There are — well, quite a few matters actually, relating to your aunt's estate I need to discuss with you. Perhaps you could make an appointment?'

'Yes, yes of course, Jo — er Mr Smethurst.' I matched formality for formality in my reply. 'I could make it in my lunch hour — say tomorrow — if that is convenient for you?'

When my rumbling stomach the following day reminded me that I was forgoing lunch to keep my appointment and had not eaten a larger breakfast to compensate, I wished I had suggested another time. When he asked his secretary to bring in coffee I hoped he hadn't heard my protesting digestive system, but was gratified to see a plate of biscuits on the tray when it arrived.

'As you know we have been your aunt's solicitors for a long time and she also appointed us as the executors of her will. I must apologize for the delay in getting things

— er — settled but it has been more complicated than we expected, mainly due to — er — the unfortunate circumstances of your aunt's death.' *Well*, I thought to myself, *unfortunate circumstance is one way of describing a murder*. 'No doubt as her only surviving relative you — er — had — well . . . expectations?'

I sat up straighter and glared at him across the desk, what was he suggesting and why couldn't he manage at least one sentence without an *er* in it?

'No, Mr Smethurst, I did not have any expectations. Grace has been more than generous to me over the years. She took me in, educated me, and more than that she gave me a home and — and love. Without her I should have spent my childhood in an institution.'

'Yes, yes, Miss — er — Please don't agitate yourself. I can assure you I did not mean to imply — I just wished to acquaint you with the salient facts. As it happens she had originally left the bulk of her estate to her friend, Tom Ensley, your employer. Quite recently she came in and said she wished to change this. She told me she was prepared to leave him his shop premises, but the residue of her estate, which is considerable, is parcelled out between you and one other person who — as yet — we have not located.'

'Do you mean,' I asked, 'Grace owned Tom's shop — the building I mean?'

Josh Smethurst looked slightly irritated at this interruption. 'That is correct, but he only gets it when the bequests to you and this other person have been paid.'

'And you have not been able to locate the other person?'

'That is correct,' he repeated.

'How much — I mean, what does her estate amount to?' I felt colour rising up my neck; after claiming I was not interested in anything my aunt had left I was now asking how much.

'The shop premises and its contents together with the flat above and its contents, and some other property. Plus, of course, the copyright in her novels. She arranged that with her publisher and agent quite separately from her will, and you already know about that. One of the reasons I wished to see you is to hand this over; it arrived a few days ago from her publisher.' He leaned across the desk and passed me a sheet of paper. I saw that it was a royalty statement; a cheque was pinned to it.

'But this is six hundred pounds!' I gasped.

'I understand you receive some remuneration every six months. Not quite enough to live on, I am afraid,' he added with a rueful smile.

To me it was an unexpected bonanza. 'This — this other person — who is it? Could I see a copy of the will?'

Josh pursed his lips and stared at me lugubriously over the desk. 'Unfortunately we have run into a little difficulty, apart from not, at the moment, knowing the whereabouts of the other legatee, we do not have a signed copy of your aunt's last will in our possession. Because we have been her lawyers for so many years we are aware of her wishes and know that she was very anxious to change her will in your favour, so we are playing for time. We hope you can help us find the other legatee, and, what is even more important, may have some idea where your aunt could have put the other copy of the will.'

I stared at him; 'But didn't she sign it here? Surely you must have a copy?'

'We have a copy yes — but unsigned. She took one copy home with her, said she would read it through that night, get it signed and bring it back the following day.' He stared at me unhappily, then, with lowered gaze and voice, he added, 'She was killed that night. So we have an unsigned copy of her will here and there is probably a signed copy somewhere else. If we cannot find it we shall have no alternative other than adhere to the original will. This is her new one.' He handed over an imposing-looking legal document to me, I stared at it in total bewilderment, wondering if I were going insane. The name of the other beneficiary was Derek Royle.

20

I felt my mouth open but at first no sound came out. I tried again and, in a voice that didn't sound in the least like my own, I grated, 'A person who goes by that name lives next door to me.'

'Next door to you — are you sure?' Josh sounded incredulous.

'Well, I'm quite sure that he lives next door, equally sure that that is what he calls himself. But he could be using that name . . . it may not be his own . . . ' My voice trailed away. What was I accusing Derek of doing or being? 'He has his six-year-old nephew staying with him at the moment because his sister is in hospital, at least that is what he told me . . . ' I was gabbling and making things sound worse for Derek with every word as I grappled with the information I had just been given and attempted to make sense of it. Josh must have got something wrong I thought. Derek Royle could not possibly be mentioned in Grace's will — they didn't even know one another. Or did they?

'There must be some mistake,' I muttered at last.

'No mistake.' Josh indicated the will. 'You can see for yourself.' He passed the will back to me so that I could take a second look.

I reached across the desk and all but snatched it from his outstretched hand. Then the name leapt out at me a second time; there really was no mistake. 'It says she has left him the shop,' I mumbled half-aloud as I read, 'the business, the goodwill and the contents. Is that correct?' It sounded as if I minded, but I had only said it for something to say.

'Yes, quite correct.' I looked up and met his gaze 'Did you — were you . . . ?' His voice tailed off as if he had reservations about voicing his thoughts.

I shook my head. 'No, I never expected to inherit her business. I don't think I would really want it. To be truthful I never thought much of it and wondered how on earth she made a living from it. Of course, I know now she had other means of making money. To be honest I never thought of inheriting anything because I never thought about Grace dying — stupid of me, I suppose. After all, as they say, only two things are certain in life, death and taxes.' I knew I was gabbling again; there was something I wanted to ask but somehow it seemed difficult after just saying I had never thought about inheriting anything from my aunt. Josh Smethurst, however, seemed to pick up my thoughts. I turned my attention back to the document in my hand.

' 'My flat and its contents, as well as the copyright in my novels goes to Angela Divine, known as my niece, as does my other property, eventually.' What does she mean?' I asked.

'The bookshop — the building, that is. It is only left to Tom Ensley for his lifetime. On his death that, too, becomes yours.' He hesitated before continuing. 'Should you predecease him then your inheritance goes to him.' He looked at me as if that concerned him. 'I intended asking her to change that when she brought the draft she had taken to study back for our safe-keeping.'

'I see,' I murmured doubtfully when I had worked out what predecease actually meant. 'And the book business?'

'Oh, that was nothing to do with Grace; that is entirely Tom's affair. She just owned the building and let him have it at a peppercorn rent.'

'A what?'

'Peppercorn rent — that means he virtually had it for nothing — just a token payment, a dollar, a quid, a euro, something like that, just so that he was legally the tenant.'

'I see,' I murmured, wondering if the legal world would ever make sense to me. 'What happens now?'

216

'Now we know where Derek Royle is hiding we get him in here and acquaint him with the facts.'

'I don't think he's actually hiding,' I protested, 'I mean, he made no secret of his name to me — it just didn't mean anything to me.'

'Would you happen to have his phone number?' Josh suppressed a thin smile at my reaction.

'Yes, I do.' I rummaged in my wallet and produced a scrap of paper with a mobile number scrawled on it. Derek had given it to me 'just in case'.

Josh copied it to a notepad. 'Thanks very much — I'll be in touch with him,' he told me as he passed the paper back. I got to my feet ready to leave. I myself wanted a word with Derek, to find out why he had never told me that he had any connection with my aunt. I was tempted to go straight home and bang on his door but a glance at my watch told me that my lunch hour was almost over. Maybe it would be better to consider this turn of events before I talked to him, I thought, as I walked back to the shop.

Curiosity however got the better of discretion. Pulling a face at the cup of instant coffee I had made before the water boiled and to which I had added milk too generously, I pulled my mobile out of my bag and, with the scrap of paper in my other hand, dialled the number. I got the engaged signal. Obviously Josh had got in first. For some reason this disturbed me. I wasn't quite sure why, but I would have liked to get in touch with Derek before the lawyer did. I clicked my phone off, returned it to my handbag, and went into the shop intending to apologize to Tom for being late, but he was busy with a customer. In fact he was more than busy: he was so engrossed in what the man, whose back was towards me, had to say that my return went unnoticed. I moved over to the area grandly called the office, in reality little more than an alcove, and sat down in front of the computer. There was a list of books I needed to check. I glanced up when I heard the door, expecting to see a new customer, but it was the person who had been talking to Tom and was now leaving. My hands froze on the keys, it was Malcolm. What on earth had he had to say to Tom that had held their attention in such a grip that neither of them noticed me?

My mind seethed with questions, but with Christmas so close the shop was busy and I had no chance to ask Tom any of them. Just before the end of the day he called out to me, 'Would you mind locking up? I have an appointment.' He only offered this explanation when he saw that I looked surprised; Tom always liked to lock up himself and check that everything was in order.

'Yes, yes of course,' I agreed, then I thought about the till and the day's takings. 'But — '

'I'll call back in later this evening,' he told me, guessing what was on my mind.

'Come on, Billy!' I hustled the little dog on his way. Walking to and from the shop was something I did to give him exercise. I felt rather noble about it this evening, as it was dark and cold with freezing fog lingering in the air. It was a relief to reach my own front door. Derek's flat was shrouded in darkness. I told myself he was probably in the back and banged hard on his door. There was no response, nothing but a silence dense enough to convince me no one was at home. I didn't know whether to be relieved or sorry when I turned away to the comfort and warmth of my own flat.

The light was blinking on my Answerphone when I let myself in. There were two messages. All I could hear on one was heavy breathing, at least it sounded like that, followed by the click as the call was terminated. I pressed the button to collect the second message. It was Malcolm.

'How about meeting me for a pre-Christmas drink? The Green Man at seven? No need to bother to ring me back — just turn up or not as the case may be. I'll be there till eight o'clock.' I was irritated at what seemed an arrogant summons and decided to stay at home. As I finished listening to it there was a faint sound behind me. My first reaction was that Billy had made the noise, but he was standing quite still, his head cocked, as he stared at the door. I caught my breath and gave a slight shudder as something like fear rippled up my spine. Then I noticed the folded note that had been pushed under the door. I had stepped over it in the dark when I came in. Now, with the lights on, it was clearly visible. I unfolded the paper and read: *Taken Jimmy to meet Santa and view the Christmas lights. See you later. Take care!*

It was an innocuous and friendly message, but as I stared down at it in my hand I got the feeling that it was not as casual as it would seem. I gave myself a mental shake and told myself I was being neurotic. *Take care* was the sort of thing people were always saying to one another, it didn't mean anything out of the ordinary. He said he would see me later, presumably when he got home from being a good uncle. I would be able to confront him then and find out why he had never mentioned that he knew Grace. Knew her pretty well too, it would seem. Irrationally cross with Derek for not being home I toyed with the idea of taking Malcolm up on his invitation. I went to my room, redid my make-up and hair and changed into something warm enough to withstand the weather outside. Then I fed Billy and gave myself a toasted cheese sandwich. Feeling restless I decided to leave it to fate: if Derek turned up in the next half-hour or so then I wouldn't go; if not then I would walk the short distance to the Green Man.

He hadn't shown up and, as I stepped out into the unpleasant cold and clammy night air, I wondered what on earth I was doing and for a moment I thought of turning back inside. I suppressed the twinge about leaving Billy but smiled to myself as I imagined Malcolm's expression if I arrived in the pub with him in tow. Besides, my curiosity was piqued by that earnest conversation I had witnessed him having with Tom. Had Malcolm really not known I was there?'

The Green Man was my 'local' — literally just round the corner, so I was pushing open its door a few minutes after closing my own. I saw Malcolm immediately; he was watching for me and he leapt up immediately, a great contrast to his behaviour in the shop.

While I waited for him to get our drinks at the bar I thought about Derek's message and wondered if it really had been there when I arrived home. I remembered Billy looking at the bottom of the door as if he had been watching something, maybe a piece of folded paper being pushed underneath.

'Penny for them?' Malcolm said, as he passed me the glass of white wine I had asked for. 'You were miles away, sitting there frowning to yourself — must have been pretty heavy thoughts.'

I gave myself a shake. 'I . . . ' I began, then stopped. 'I was thinking about Grace,' I lied, wondering why I didn't simply tell Malcolm what was really bothering me.

He reached over and put his hand on mine. 'Don't . . . ' he admonished. 'Try to forget it all now; you can't put the clock back. The time has come to look to the future.'

'But not forget the past.' I slid my hand from beneath his to lift my glass to my lips. Fleetingly I wondered why Malcolm was going out of his way to be so nice. I dismissed the thought as quickly as it came. He was just being normal — the Malcolm I had known — or thought I knew — before all this ghastly business of Grace's death. I smiled at him and pushed the thought of Derek to the back of my mind.

I was just picking up my second drink when I became aware that I was under observation. Responding to the urge to turn round I saw a young woman on the other side of the room staring at me intently. I wondered if I knew her: was she an old school-friend perhaps? For a few seconds our gazes locked and held. There was something familiar about her, but the impression was fleeting. I decided I had never seen her before. Her close scrutiny made me uncomfortable and I turned back to Malcolm who was offering me another refill.

I shook my head, 'I haven't started this one!' I protested, conscious that I was already beginning to feel light headed, no doubt because I had eaten very little during the day.

'How about dinner then? I'll check at the bar that we can get a table.' He returned with another drink, ignoring my protests and took it for granted that I would stay and have dinner with him. Feeling pleasantly hazy and relaxed I let myself go with the flow — after all I had nothing else to do, no one else to see, and I was hungry.

'Drink up then we had better claim our table before someone else does.'

'You go ahead — I just need to freshen up before we eat. Take my drink in with you.' As I stood up the woman on the other side of the room got up too. I saw her speak to her companion before she followed me towards the ladies' room.

Sudden panic speeded me up; once through the outer door I locked myself in a stall. Certain now that the stranger did have an interest in me I heard the outer door open and close and the click of heels; what I didn't hear was the opening and closing of another stall door, which meant that the stranger was waiting for me to emerge. With the prospect of spending the remainder of the evening skulking in a toilet or facing her it did not take me long to make up my mind. I flushed the toilet and, taking a deep breath, opened the door and walked briskly across to the washbasins. I studied the other woman in the mirror as I washed my hands. Aware that I couldn't go on doing this for ever I eventually turned round;

'Do I know you?' I pulled a paper towel out of the dispenser with an angry jerk.

She shook her head. 'No, but I know of you. You are Angela Divine whose aunt was murdered recently. From what I remember of her she was a nice lady and I was very sorry.'

'You knew Grace?'

'I haven't seen her since I was a small child, but I remember her as a nice person. My brother was very fond of her. It was pretty tough for him having to identify her body as soon as he got here to visit her.'

'Your brother identified the body?' I repeated the words with a feeling that the pieces of the jigsaw were dropping into place. The mystery stepson — but no — it couldn't be. 'Who is your brother?' The question came out in a hoarse croak.

'I thought you knew him — Derek Royle. My little boy is staying with him at the moment and has talked about you, you and your dog.'

I blurted the only words that came to my mind; 'Then Jimmy is your little boy?' before I remembered. 'But you are in hospital — that's why Derek has Jimmy.'

'Is that what he told you?' She laughed, 'Just for the record, what is the matter with me?'

'I — I don't know.' I spoke the simple truth, I supposed Derek had told me what was, or what was supposed to be, the reason for his sister being in hospital but even if my life depended on it I could not remember. All I was aware of was a rising annoyance, no that was far too mild a word, rage was more like it, that Derek had lied to me, not once, it seemed, but consistently.

I remembered I had left Malcolm claiming our table for dinner and realized I couldn't stay much longer here in the ladies or he would send in a search party for me. I was so angry with Derek that the prospect of sitting through a dinner with Malcolm looked like a good idea. I told myself I didn't care if I never saw Derek again; in fact I hoped I never would. I had temporarily forgotten that I planned to spend most of Christmas Day with him.

'Nice to have met you,' I said rather insincerely, 'but I had better go now — my companion will be waiting.'

'Nice to have met you too.' She sounded much more genuine than I had. 'I expect I'll see you again. 'Bye for now — I must rescue Derek from Jimmy now. He took him to see Santa while I did some shopping on my own.' Her smile was warm and friendly as she left.

Malcolm scowled. 'You took a long time;' he complained. 'You obviously met a friend in there. Who was it?'

'She was not a friend; in fact I don't know her all,' I snapped, rubbed up the wrong way by his tone. 'She claims to know me and also claims to have known Grace.' I peered past Malcolm to the menu on the blackboard behind him, determined to concentrate on anything other than Derek or his sister and, at the same time, let Malcolm know that as far as I was concerned there was nothing more to be said on the subject.

21

'Don't be ridiculous,' I protested, 'my flat is only just round the corner, there is no need to run me home.'

'Don't you be ridiculous,' Malcolm retaliated. 'I can't let you walk and I drive past your door.' Reluctantly I got in to the car, only to protest even more vehemently a short while later.

'What are you doing? Where are you going? You've passed my flat.' I peered round, realizing that the street we had turned into was unfamiliar. 'This isn't where I live.'

Malcolm half-turned in his seat to face me as he switched off the engine. 'No, it isn't,' he agreed. 'It is where I live.'

'But . . . 'I stammered. 'I thought . . . 'I tailed off again. What exactly had I thought? I had always assumed that he lived with his parents — was he taking me to meet them? But he had asked me to do that on Christmas Night. I wished I had drunk a little less wine, I might be thinking a bit more clearly now. 'Are you taking me to meet your parents?' I asked hopefully.

'No,' he answered shortly. 'My parents

don't live here with me. This is my own place.' In the light of the streetlamps I could see that he was amused. 'What did you think I was doing, taking you to see them to get their approval?' His voice was mocking, making me feel gauche. He was getting out of the car as he spoke and I realized I was expected to do the same. I hesitated, not convinced I liked the idea of being alone with him.

'Are you going to sit there all night?' I could hear both sardonic amusement and impatience in his voice, so I climbed slowly out of the car instead of answering 'Yes.' He took my elbow, making escape difficult if not impossible as he led me to the entrance of the small block of flats.

The small vestibule was reasonably lit and warm but the shiver I gave had nothing to do with physical chill. Malcolm gestured to the wide steps. 'I am on the first floor.'

I began to climb, there seemed nothing else to do with Malcolm a step or two behind me and a locked door behind him. As I waited for him at the door to his own flat and watched him select the correct key on the ring and fit it into the lock I wondered why I was so tense. This was only Malcolm, whom I knew, not some faceless nameless stranger, yet as I heard the lock click and he pushed open the door, the voice in my head was murmuring *Will you walk into my parlour said the spider to the fly?*

I'm getting paranoid, I thought, as he clicked a switch and the room was illuminated. I looked round and saw quite an ordinary lounge: nothing like a spider's web, nothing sinister at all, in fact. It was furnished comfortably and conventionally with a three-piece suite and several small tables. A counter, somewhat reminiscent of a public bar, cut off one corner; behind it I could see coffee-making facilities, a microwave and a small sink. I took in all this while Malcolm moved round the room switching on a couple of lamps and turning off the main light. It was clean, tidy, functional and, as far as I could see, totally unlived-in. It was this last fact that made me uneasy.

'You are not cold, are you?' Malcolm's voice was solicitous. I shook my head; hardly, I thought. If anything the room felt overheated. 'Then take your coat off and make yourself at home while I fix us a drink.' Obediently I shrugged out of my outdoor things and tossed them over the back of one of the chairs before sitting down on the overstuffed sofa. Malcolm meanwhile was collecting glasses and bottles from the cupboards beneath the counter top.

He hadn't asked me what I would like, or even if I wanted a drink, but handed me a wineglass filled with some sparkling pinkish liquid. A slice of lemon was perched on the rim and a maraschino cherry impaled on a toothpick acted as a swizzlestick.

'A Christmas cocktail,' he said, handing it to me before I had time to ask what it was. It looked not only innocuous but enticing, I thought, as I accepted it.

It was sweet, but not too sweet and had a pleasant but definite zing. I drained my glass and popped the cherry in my mouth. 'Ummm nice,' I murmured, feeling more relaxed than I had all day.

'I'll get you another.' Malcolm whipped the glass from my hand and disappeared behind the bar. I smiled. 'Thanks!' I said as I took the second glass from his outstretched hand. Leaning back against the cushions I raised the glass to my lips. I wondered what was in it and tried to ask, but I was so tired it was hard to form the words or even to think what it was I wanted to know. I looked up at Malcolm. He was standing in front of me, swaying. I tried to ask him to keep still but couldn't find the words, nor could I keep my eyes open. My lids drooped, so did my wrist and Malcolm just caught my glass before it fell to the floor.

It was a very odd sensation. I was aware of Malcolm's voice but seemed unable to focus my attention on him or to answer him coherently. I felt him shake my arm, or thought I did, and heard his voice, crisp and commanding. 'Come on now — where is it?'

'Where is what?' I tried to ask, but my tongue felt stiff and swollen; I was unable to get round the words or get them out. I felt the grip on my arm tighten painfully, and heard Malcolm's voice as from a great distance repeating his question. I shook my head. 'I don't know what you are talking about,' I mumbled through the fog that was closing in; I had the impression that someone was going through the contents of my handbag; then, unable to fight any longer, I simply let go.

★ ★ ★

'Ugh!' Moaning and raising my hands to my pounding head I tried to sit up. That was when I discovered I was no longer on the overpadded couch but lying on a bed. The only light coming into the room was from the streetlamps outside, and that only crept in where the curtains failed to meet. With a supreme effort I pulled myself up into a sitting position and, as my eyes grew accustomed to the dim light, I saw the outline of a table lamp on the bedside table. Reaching, I fumbled for the switch; to my relief it came on. It did not exactly flood the room with brilliance, obviously the globe was of a very low wattage, but it was certainly a great improvement and in its light I saw a piece of paper on the bedside table, It was folded over and on the up side I could see my name, printed in large capitals. I picked the paper up and unfolded it with shaky fingers that were unwilling to do my bidding. The message was brief but obviously intended for me.

Sorry, you should have at least tried to be co-operative — as it was you left me no alternative.

I read it through again — and again — trying to gather my scrambled wits and work out exactly what the words meant.

My head throbbed with a dull persistent beat; I had a disconnected feeling and my tongue felt at least twice its normal size, I craved for a long cool drink, preferably iced. I moved across to the door on legs which, like my tongue, felt oversized. I tried the knob; as I had guessed, the door was locked. There was another door in the room, which did open under my hand. I groped round and found a light switch. I was in a well-appointed bathroom; an upturned tumbler was by the washbasin; so at least I could drink.

I filled the glass to overflowing with blissfully cool water and drank it down in one long gasp. After a deep sigh I refilled it and this time drank slowly, savouring its reviving and refreshing quality. Never had I appreciated plain water so much and in that moment was sure I would never want to drink anything else. Looking round, I noticed a bath sponge on the far end of the tub. I held it under the cold tap, squeezed out the excess and dabbed my face before holding it first against my temples then on the back of my neck, just below my hairline. The effect was magical; I shook my head several times and with the action felt the dull haze in my head disperse marginally.

This small physical recovery was swiftly replaced by emotional turmoil: a cauldron of emotions that gradually unified into blind fury. How on earth had I let myself get into such an indefensible position?

A further check of my surroundings confirmed that there was no escape. Hammering on the door was useless, there did not appear to be anyone in the building to hear or, if they heard, to care, and rattling the doorknob only served to confirm that it was locked. Back in the bathroom I clambered up precariously on the end of the bath; the frosted window was also locked. Even if I broke the glass it was probably too small for me to get through and anyway I remembered the apartment was not on the ground floor. I clambered down, slumped on the bed and gave way to tears of frustration and self-pity.

The ringing of a phone jerked me back to the present moment. I looked round; there was no phone in sight, then I realized it was coming from my own handbag.

I snatched it up and pressed it to my ear. 'Hello — hello — who is it?' There was a tremor in my voice and I sounded as if I were suffering from a head cold after my emotional storm. There was a pause — then a sort of crackle — then another pause before a familiar voice asked:

'Angie, Is that you?'

My grip tightened on the instrument in my hand, my breath caught in my throat and an icy finger of terror crawled down my spine.

'Grace?' The single word came out as a harsh croak before the room swam round me, the phone slipped from my fingers and I fell back on the bed in a dead faint.

When I surfaced I forced myself to think clearly. Of course it could not be Grace; it must be someone imitating her. Someone who was a good mimic. I remembered Malcolm telling me how he enjoyed amateur dramatics and had always played female parts at his all-boys' school.

No doubt this was why I had been left my mobile; he probably thought this cruel deception would freak me out completely. Well it had — temporarily — and I still had my mobile phone. Determined not to be beaten I scrolled through my contacts then stopped; whom among them could I trust? I paused on Derek's number. Could I — dare I — trust him? I had to take the risk; the prospect of being left here till Malcolm — or someone else — released me was more than I wished to contemplate. Grace's number was still in my contacts list; I had never got around to deleting it. For one crazy moment I wondered: could that have been her voice, or had I been hallucinating? Finger poised I hesitated before pressing the key that would call Grace's number.

It only took a shocked second to realize when the call was answered that it was her answering service.

I did my best to get some sense and clarity into my thoughts. The memory that Grace's phone had been disconnected shook me, then I realized it was her mobile I had called. Obviously it was still viable, but where was it?

I shook my head as if the action might shake my scattered wits together, then gulped more of the cold water. Thirst still plagued me. At last I came to the conclusion that I had to take a risk: follow my gut feeling; I must reach someone I could trust. I ran through my contacts again and clicked on Derek's number. When it was answered I recognized the voice immediately; the only thing was, it didn't belong to Derek. Shocked into silence when I realized it was Malcolm I terminated the call. I must have clicked on the wrong name; they were next to each other in my contacts list. Slowly, carefully, using every iota of concentration I still possessed I tried again. This time I was sure I had made no mistake.

'Kind of me to leave your phone with you, don't you think?'

I was not sure how to reply or even what to reply. 'Why did you?' I blurted at last. Somehow I didn't think kindness came into the equation.

'So that we could talk — you and I.' There was a pause, then, 'I had to do some manipulating with your contacts' numbers. But I thought you would like hearing your aunt's voice once more.' His voice was cool and expressionless. At least I knew now why, when I dialled Derek's number, I got

Malcolm. I felt a surge of relief; it was the numbers he had played with, it didn't mean something terrible had happened to Derek.

I felt the now familiar ripple of fear skitter down my spine but managed to say, as firmly as possible, 'Would you please let me out of here?' In spite of my best efforts I could not control the tremor in my voice. 'I — I want to go home, Malcolm.' Then, suddenly unsure about his explanation of the changed numbers, I stammered, 'Where are you — I dialled Derek's number?'

'You did?' The mocking tone in his voice chilled me. 'Then I guess that is where I am — in Derek's flat. I will let him confirm this.'

A few moments later I heard Derek. 'Angie — are you OK?' Before I could respond, Malcolm cut in, 'Of course she is OK. Don't ask her again. Just give her my instructions.'

After a brief pause Derek spoke again.

'Just tell him what he wants to know.' It was Derek's voice but he sounded as if he was under some sort of pressure.

If only I knew what it was he wanted to know or, more important, that I would be able to give him the answer he wanted.

'Did you get that?' Malcolm was back on the line. 'You are the one who should be answering questions — not me,' he continued. 'Now answer me and tell me what I need to know.'

'I don't know what you want to know, truly I don't.' Tears of fear and frustration filled my voice. 'I can't tell you because I don't know what you want to know.' I heard something very like the shrill yip of a small dog in distress.

'Is that Billy?'

'If that is what that scruffy little cur is called — yes.'

'What are you doing to him?' I demanded.

'Nothing — yet.' I heard a muffled yelp over the phone. 'But I might unless you are co-operative.'

My concern for the little dog as well as fear for myself sent another shudder of fear through me. 'What *do* you want to know?' I asked in as firm a voice as I could muster.

'Where has your aunt hidden them?'

'Hidden what?'

'Don't play games with me, Angie. Her important documents — just where are they?'

'I don't know anything about any documents — I suppose everything is lodged with the lawyers.'

'Not the ones I want. Someone knows where they are and I think that someone is you.'

'I don't know anything about any papers other than those with the lawyers,' I protested.

A shrill yelp rang in my ear. 'I know how fond you are of Billy . . . ' Malcolm's voice was quiet but none the less frightening for all that. 'So maybe you had better think — and think hard — because if anyone knows you do.'

22

The phone went dead. I stared at it in my hand for a moment, still trying to work out how I had been connected to Malcolm when it had been Derek's number I had called and whether I had imagined it and therefore had been totally deranged when I heard Grace's voice. For a wild moment. I even allowed the possibility that I might be dead myself and that was how I had been talking to Grace. I had just dismissed that idea as totally impossible when the phone rang again.

Heart thumping in trepidation, I answered it with a breathless 'Hello' expecting to hear Malcolm's voice and half-afraid, half-hoping, that it might be Grace. It was neither.

'Angie?' Derek sounded strained, unlike himself. I had a vision of him with a gun at his head.

'Yes?' I croaked.

'Listen and listen good. Think; there must be somewhere — in the flat perhaps, where Grace kept things — important papers. Can you think of anywhere?'

'Derek, is . . . ?' The phone went silent. I wanted to know if Billy was OK. I knew

Malcolm had never liked him but surely he wouldn't do anything to the little dog to get at me? I wondered how Derek had managed to phone me, or had he been forced to? I wished I did know something that might persuade Malcolm to release me from my prison. I lay back on the bed, closed my eyes and willed my mind to go back — to remember.

I travelled mentally to the time Grace had first taken me away from the school after my parents' death. With eyes closed I dredged my memory bank. All I could recapture was that dreadful feeling of loss and aloneness.

With the painful memory flooded a renewed realization of what I had lost so much more recently. Grace had been more than an aunt to me; she had been my entire family and a wonderful friend. I was overcome with remorse as I remembered how we had agreed I needed my own place — my own space. If only I had remained with Grace in her flat. I took a deep breath: the 'If only' path was no way to go, I had moved out — I had wanted to be independent, and Grace was dead, whatever I had heard, or imagined I had heard, on the phone. I reminded myself why I was taking this painful trip down memory lane, closed my eyes and did my best to think, to remember something — anything

— that might be useful.

With a jolt my head shot up. I had momentarily dropped off, or at least nearly so, but struggling to surface was another memory — right back on that first night with my aunt . . .

★ ★ ★

I didn't know whether it was some sound in the flat or my dream that roused me. I woke up unsure where I was and why, I was also very thirsty. Still half-asleep I slid out of bed. The room was dimly lit as Grace, understanding that I might be suffering from night terrors after the shock of the day, had left a night-light burning. I saw a line of light under another door; I could not remember the layout of the flat, and could not work out whether it was the lounge, the kitchen or the bathroom.

I opened the door; it was none of those, but Grace's bedroom. My aunt was standing on her bed fiddling with a painting on the wall; at least that was what I first thought, but, as I stood there, I saw what appeared to be a hole in the wall. Grace pulled a little door shut over it — I can remember the click it made — swung the painting back into place and got carefully down off the bed. Only then did she notice me watching from the doorway.

'Angie!' Her voice was sharp and for a moment I was afraid I had made her angry, but she added in a softer tone, 'Good gracious — you startled me. I — I was just putting that picture straight — didn't want it to drop on my head in the night!' She gave a little laugh. Only now, recalling the incident after all these years, do I remember the brief glimpse I had at the time of the small door being clicked shut before the picture was pulled back over it. Being more concerned with finding a drink of water and seeing no significance in it at the time, I had accepted at face value Grace's explanation that she was simply straightening the painting before it dropped on her head.

'Couldn't you sleep?' Grace enquired kindly, leading me from the room towards the kitchen. 'No, I don't suppose you could.'

'I wanted a drink. I was asleep and I woke up thirsty,' I explained.

Grace poured me a glass of cool fruit juice from the fridge. I would rather have had water but didn't want to complain when she was being so kind. She took me back to bed and tucked me in when I had drunk the juice, pointing out that it was well after midnight.

★   ★   ★

Not even properly awake at the time, I had accepted my aunt's explanation about the painting at face value. Now I was convinced that I had remembered the incident correctly and in its entirety, I knew that what I had seen was my aunt closing a hidden safe in her bedroom. Was this the information I needed to trade for my freedom? I looked round for my mobile, then paused, uncertain what number I should dial. Or even whom I wanted to speak to — whom could I trust?

Remembering the last time I had use my mobile I reflected bitterly that it really didn't seem to matter what number I dialled — I always got Malcolm. I punched in Derek's number.

As I had half-expected it was Malcolm who replied. 'Well?' he barked, 'I hope for everyone's sake you have been thinking — and thinking hard.'

'Yes I have,' I told him. 'I have remembered the very first night Grace brought me home, after she collected me from school and broke the news to me about my parents — '

'Yes, yes, go on — get to the point,' Malcolm interrupted in a gruff voice.

'Well, I woke up some time in the night feeling thirsty and went out of my room in search of a drink. I was half-asleep and couldn't remember which was the bathroom door, I was just going to get myself some water in the glass I had seen in there — '

'Just get to the point,' Malcolm snarled again.

'I wasn't quite sure which door it was and opened the wrong one — the door to Grace's bedroom. She was standing on the bed fiddling with a painting. I thought she must be straightening it, then I saw the hole in the wall. As I watched she slammed a little door shut over it and swung the picture back in place. I had forgotten all about it till now. She helped me get a drink and took me back to bed. I never thought about it again till — well, till just now.'

'Why the hell couldn't you have told someone about this before?'

'No one asked me, and anyway I had forgotten about it till I really thought hard and made myself remember.' I decided to push my luck. 'Now that I have told you will you let me go?'

My request prompted a cynical laugh, 'Not on your life — you could have made it up. When I've got what I want — maybe.' I felt that now familiar *frisson* of fear ripple down my spine at the words and the tone in which they were delivered. 'Tell you what, as a reward I'll let this pesky little dog go, then you won't have to worry that I might do something to him. Which I might if he irritates me enough.'

'You can't do that — you can't just throw him out in the street, not at night. Anything might happen to him!'

'It will if I have to put up with him much longer, but if you co-operate I'll let you have him back.' The phone went abruptly dead.

What happened next took me completely by surprise. About fifteen minutes later I heard a key turning in the lock. Instinctively I froze.

'Billy!' I gasped in astonishment, as the little dog was dropped on the floor just inside the door. Derek followed him, not quite so precipitously.

'Derek!' I gasped 'What on earth are you doing?'

He put his finger to his lips before snarling, 'Here's your bloody dog. I hope you enjoy his company.'

Then, in an action that seemed as out of place as the finger-to-lips gesture, he winked. He definitely winked. It was as puzzling as the growl in his voice. I stared as the door closed behind him and waited to hear the click of the lock. It didn't come. Only when I heard the outer door close did I put my hand tentatively on the knob and even more cautiously turn it. The door was not locked.

My first impulse was to fling the door wide and race out of my prison. Then the thought occurred to me that it might well be some sort of trick and I would only be caught as soon as, if not before, I left the building. My heart thumped in my chest with fear and anxiety. I crossed the room and sat down on the bed while I wondered what to do, where to go.

Malcolm was the one who had locked me in here, but Derek's behaviour seemed so bizarre I doubted if he were to be trusted either. Then I thought of Tom. Yes, of course. If I could get to the shop he would help me. That was the thing I must do; now that I had Billy safe there was no need to go home and rescue him. Even though it was night and the shop would be closed, I had my own key in my handbag, and if I locked myself in there for the night I would be quite safe until Tom arrived in the morning to open up.

My courage and resolve bolstered by this plan, I cautiously opened the door and peered out on to the empty and silent landing. Snatched up my handbag, tucked Billy under my arm and, as fast as I could without abandoning caution, I tiptoed down the stairs and out into the street. I realized I was less than half a mile from the shop premises. What luck!

I could feel my heart hammering against my ribs and my breath was coming in sharp spurts. Having no lead and afraid that the little dog might not stay with me I had him still tucked under my arm. With relief I slumped against the wall by the back entrance to the shop and fumbled in my bag for the keys I always kept there. My hand shook as I struggled to fit them into the lock, then, with a feeling of unutterable relief, I let the door swing shut behind me. I stepped out of the small back hallway into the kitchen, wondering why the lights were on.

'Tom!' I exclaimed, seeing my employer sitting at the table watching the door as I burst through it. 'What are you doing here?' It didn't strike me that he had more right to be there than myself. 'Am I glad to see you! I don't think I could stand being on my own much longer. You have no idea how scared I've been — then I thought I could get here — that was when I discovered I could get out. I never thought you would be here at this time of night . . . ' I slowly puttered to a stop like a dying engine, as I realized that he had not responded to my outpouring but was merely sitting — quite still — staring at me. This totally unnerved me and I felt the now all-too-familiar prickle of sheer terror. I had never imagined the day would come when

Tom could engender such a feeling. He simply sat and stared at me, his eyes cold and his lips unsmiling. As my torrent of words petered out I stared back at him, as silent as he was. I wanted to ask again what he was doing here, but as I stared he answered my question. Spoken in a different tone of voice it would have comforted me, but when he answered, 'Waiting for you', it only tightened the icy fear that held me in its grip.

I managed to croak, 'What for?' Then, as another thought struck me, 'How did you know I was coming?'

Tom shrugged. 'I didn't know, I deduced.'

'Deduced?' I repeated the word as if I didn't understand it. 'Deduced what?' I stammered, my voice a mere croak.

'That you would decide this was the only safe place to go to when you — er — escaped.' The thin line his lips had set into twitched slightly, not enough to be a smile, certainly not enough to give me any comfort.

'I . . . see,' I murmured, although I didn't see at all. 'How did you know I would escape? Come to that, how did you know I was somewhere I needed to escape from?'

'An educated guess. Very educated.' The last two words, added as emphasis, had a sinister ring.

I stared at him, bemused. This was not the

Tom I thought I knew. This man was scary, not a bit like my kindly dreamy boss.

'Why have you brought that damned dog here?' The question alerted me to the fact that I was still clutching Billy under my arm, rather too tightly for his comfort if his wriggling was anything to go by. I put him down on the ground and answered simply and truthfully, 'Because I couldn't leave him there.'

'Leave him where?'

Convinced that he knew perfectly well exactly where both Billy and I had come from I didn't answer.

'Leave him — where?' The question came again in a steely voice. 'Are you telling me the dog was with you?'

I nodded. 'He was brought to me because I — '

'Because you — what?' he cut in, before I could finish my sentence.

'I — I gave them some information they required.' Even as I spoke I felt I should be keeping my mouth shut.

'Which was?' I pretended not to hear, or not to understand if I had heard. Some instinct of self-preservation warned me that the less information I admitted to knowing the safer I would be. I stared blankly at the man watching me so closely and felt suffocated. I tried to take a deep breath and reached for the kitchen table to steady myself.

'You don't look too good?' Was I imagining it or was there a hint of concern in his voice? He almost sounded like the old Tom, the one I thought I knew. 'Sit down, have a cup of tea and tell me about it.'

Gratefully I sank into a chair at the table, even more gratefully accepted the mug of tea Tom pushed across the table towards me a few moments later. It was horribly strong but it did have some sort of reviving effect.

'Thank you,' I murmured, wondering whether I was awake and mad or asleep in the midst of some quite bizarre dream. I looked across the table and met his eyes on my face, the hard look seemed to have softened and his lips curved into some semblance of a smile. This was the man I had worked for and with for the last year or so. My fear abated, even seemed unreasonable, and when he asked again, 'What information had you to give?' I was ready to tell him.

'They just wanted to know if I knew of anywhere else where Grace could have hidden papers or — or anything. They promised to let me have Billy with me for company if I could remember. I thought really hard and it suddenly came to me, one of those flashes of memory that can come suddenly like a beam of light. There was a picture in my mind of the night when Grace first took me from the school to her flat.' I explained to him about the frightened child waking up thirsty and going to look for a glass of water and ending up opening the door to her aunt's bedroom instead of the bathroom. Once again I described Grace closing the door on the wall safe.

'Did you see what she put inside it? What about Grace, did she swear you to secrecy?'

'No.' I shook my head. 'She told me she was adjusting the picture, stepped down off the bed and helped me get a drink of water. I went back to bed, dropped off to sleep and forgot all about it till tonight.'

'You are sure about this — there really is a wall safe in her bedroom?'

I nodded and hoped I had not just been dreaming.

23

'You didn't dream it? Or — worse — made it up to get us off your back.'

Tom was looking at me keenly, trying to assess the truth — or otherwise — of what I had told him. I nodded, finding it difficult to speak, for the awful thing was I wasn't one hundred per cent sure; the memory had been buried for so long. I was too afraid to admit that I had any doubts and with difficulty I found my voice.

'Of course it is the truth,' I asserted, making my voice ring with righteous indignation.

He stared at me for a moment. I willed myself not to flinch or look away under his gaze. Then, getting up so suddenly from the table that he almost knocked his chair over, he said, 'I believe you, but God help you if you are lying to me.' He moved over to the door, then turned back and added, 'Wait here for me.'

It was only when he had gone that it crossed my mind that his injunction was superfluous, what choice did I have?

I was sure he would have locked me in;

even if I got out where would I go? Grace's flat was out of the question, Derek's place was equally so; I had seen enough of what I presumed was Malcolm's flat to last me for the remainder of my life and I could not expect to find safe refuge in my own flat. As I sat at the kitchen table trying to work out a plan of action with a mind suddenly made of cotton wool my eyes strayed to the door. Hanging on the hooks at the back of it alongside an umbrella was a spare lead I kept there for Billy. At least I would not have to carry him wherever I went, I thought. Listlessly I got up and retrieved it. Still with no clear plan of action I called him close and bent to click it on his collar. In doing so I noticed that the little green plastic barrel he wore round his neck was coming unscrewed. I presumed it held his name and address and was about to tighten it when some instinct — or curiosity — or maybe Grace prodding me from beyond the grave, made me pull out the paper. I told myself afterwards that I pulled it out because it needed rerolling before I could screw the two halves of the barrel firmly together. It was not, as I had thought, Billy's identity tag but a slip of paper with a six-digit number. I stared at the numbers, wondering what they represented: a phone number, perhaps? The phone ringing in the empty shop brought me back to the present moment. Quickly I rerolled the scrap of paper and replaced it in its hiding-place. I let the phone ring out. Almost immediately my mobile phone rang. This time I responded. My sense of self-preservation, or some illogical reasoning, told me this was safer. If I answered the shop phone the caller would know my whereabouts. On my mobile I could be anywhere.

'Angie?' It was Derek. I didn't know whether to be relieved or not. 'You were right about the wall safe, but it has a combination lock. No one knows what the key is.'

Of course — the number in the tag on Billy's collar. I knew with blinding clarity that I was right.

'It's six digits,' Derek went on. 'I've told them that you don't know it — how could you? — you only just remembered about the safe itself.' He was speaking in an odd tone of voice. Almost as if he was warning me not to give anyone, including himself, this information.

'You are right,' I agreed. 'How on earth would I know it? If Grace never told me about the safe she would hardly give me the combination, would she?'

'That is what I told them.' I thought I heard relief in his voice before Tom's voice took over. 'Look, girlie.' He tried to sound wheedling but calling me that certainly wasn't going to work. 'If you know that number just tell me. If you don't . . . ' his voice faded out in a sinister growl. Then I heard him say, 'See if you can get round her . . . ' and Derek was back on the line.

'Can you think of anywhere where she would put it? Think, Angie. A secret drawer somewhere — on her computer?'

Again I got the odd impression he was telling me what to say. Grasping at this small straw of comfort, I suggested, 'She could have hidden it in one of her books — that last unfinished one for instance. Maybe it is a combination of chapter numbers and page numbers, the number of words.' Remembering how my place had been broken into and pages taken from the last, unpublished manuscript Grace had written, I felt not only inspired but afraid I might be telling them the truth and not offering a red herring. I told myself this was absurd because I knew where the number was hidden; and so, I was suddenly convinced, did Derek. That thought was comforting, but did not explain what he was doing in Grace's flat with Malcolm and Tom. Neither did it explain why they were so anxious to find whatever it was she had hidden in the safe behind the picture in her bedroom.

'That's it — the secret is in that latest book of hers. We'll fire up the computer, we've got her laptop — she is sure to have the file of it saved there. We'll work on the numbers. Thanks a million, Angie. Take care of yourself and of Billy.' The last word was cut off as another voice spoke: Malcolm.

'You had better be right. I won't be able to save you — or that dog — this time,' he warned, before the phone went dead. I thought back to the earlier events of that night and thought that if knocking me out with some potent pill and leaving me locked up was Malcolm's idea of saving me then I dreaded to think of the alternative. I looked at Billy. I had his lead in my hand and he was gazing up at me expectantly and trustingly. I thought of the secret hidden on his small person, and that, more than my own safety, was the trigger that finally galvanized me into action. I pulled my phone out again with the intention of calling the police. Then the thought that they might not get here before someone else did cleared my mind and I knew that Billy and I had to get away as fast as we could.

I checked that the front door of the shop was locked and bolted from the inside, then made for the back door. As expected, Tom had locked this when he left, but he had neglected to take my keys from me. Was this an oversight, or had he suddenly been overcome with concern for me? I didn't waste time thinking about it, I let myself out into the night as quickly as I could, locked the door behind me and, urging Billy to hurry, insisting there was no time to waste on calls of nature, ran as fast as I possibly could for the police station which I knew was only a couple of streets away.

24

As I turned into the street where the police station was a car coming towards me held me in its lights for a second before I registered that it was a police car. Stupidly I turned and would have run, but Billy chose that moment to investigate an enticing smell and nearly tripped me up. I decided, or more accurately was forced, to stand still and watch two police officers leap out of the car. I immediately recognized the woman as the one I had met the day Grace died. I felt a surge of relief; she had been kind, and I just had time to wonder why I was worried anyway, after all I had been heading for the police station.

'Get in the car,' she shouted. I snatched up Billy in my arms, holding him in the tight embrace that he probably hated but I found comforting, and did as I was told. I wondered if they were arresting me.

'We were on our way to the bookshop to pick you up,' the policewoman told me.

'Oh.' Was she answering my unspoken question? The monosyllable was all I could think of to say that didn't sound incriminating. How did they know where I was?

'We had a phone call to say where you were.'

'Oh,' I repeated, feeling, and I am sure sounding, pretty stupid. I didn't need to ask who had told them.

At that moment the police radio crackled with an urgent message for the car to divert and not return to the police station. The address they were given was Grace's shop and flat.

'Looks as if we have missed the excitement,' the driver remarked laconically as we drove up and saw a couple of police cars already there. Both Tom and Malcolm were being helped into one of them by two sturdy officers of the law.

As they were driven away Derek appeared, but he wasn't under arrest, or if he was he looked very cheerful about it. He and the officer with him walked over to our car. Derek stuck his head through the window and grinned at me.

'You OK, Angie?' he asked.

I nodded, totally confused.

'Mind if I borrow Billy, or at least his tag?'

I unscrewed the little barrel and handed over the slip of paper. I knew it wasn't really Billy or his tag that was needed. I cursed myself for sitting there like a sack of potatoes instead of getting out and going into the flat with Derek and the plainclothes detective.

'See you back at the station.' Derek waved me off with a broad grin. I cleared my throat and found my voice.

'Are you — I mean, am I under arrest?' I quavered.

'Good heavens, no!' The policewoman sounded scandalized at the suggestion. She screwed round in her seat and peered at me. I must have looked even whiter and more strained than could be attributed to the effect of the streetlighting. 'Whatever made you think that?'

I felt myself slump in my seat with sheer relief. 'I'm not?' I squeaked. 'But Derek — well, he was there with them — what about him?'

She laughed. 'He certainly isn't,' she assured me. 'He is a member of the Australian Federal Police — working with us — doing an undercover job, actually.'

'He is? But — but I thought he was a journalist.'

'That's his cover. He says you've done a great job and gave him a piece of vital information tonight.'

'I did — and I have?' My confusion was growing by the minute.

Still clutching Billy to my chest, I was helped out of the car and ushered into the police station. A few minutes later another car drew up and seconds after that Derek bounded in. He was smiling and looked relieved, but there was also something else that I couldn't or dared not quite define in his face.

'Angie! Thank God you are safe!' He caught me by the shoulders and there in the vestibule of the police station in full view of everyone he kissed me. Not a full-on kiss but a kiss all the same. Poor Billy, squashed between us, wriggled and protested. 'What a joke. Billy had the vital bit of information all the time and Malcolm never guessed.' He nodded in the direction of the policeman with him. 'We tried it as soon as Tom and Malcolm had been arrested. You'll never guess what we found in the safe!'

25

'Grace's last will?' I hazarded a successful guess. He looked disappointed that I knew but quickly brightened.

'What else?'

I could see he was bursting to tell me but I didn't really care at that moment; my blood was singing with an exultation I hadn't felt for a long, long time. And it wasn't just because I was not, after all, being arrested and accused of Grace's murder.

Much later that night I snuggled up to Derek on the couch in my own lounge. Billy, who seemed to have ended up the hero of the day, was snoring on the carpet between our feet.

'Well,' I demanded, 'are you going to tell me exactly what was in that wall safe other than the will?'

'Oh, just a few documents,' Derek said airily. 'Belonging to you, I suppose.'

'Me?' I frowned, wondering what documents of mine could be there. 'What sort of documents?'

'Your birth certificate for one. A copy of Grace's final will, duly signed, for another.'

'I know about the will, and I can see why Tom at least was so desperate to stop Josh getting hold of it. Derek . . . ' I pushed myself up so that I could look into his face, 'you were mentioned in her last will. Josh Smethurst showed me a copy.' My voice died away as the truth dawned on me. 'Just who are you?' I demanded. 'The police told me that her stepson would be identifying Grace, but I didn't think she had a stepson — or any children for that matter. If she had a stepson where on earth did he vanish to?' I looked him squarely in the eye. 'Could it be you?'

'In a way.' I tutted in exasperation; how could anyone be a stepson *in a way?* Then he went on to explain, 'She also had a daughter.'

'Well, where are they now? Where is this stepson, and if he exists why have I never heard about him, or the daughter for that matter?' I felt totally confused and felt I was losing the plot — or Derek was.

'I can only suppose your aunt had her own reasons for keeping silent. No doubt she would have told you eventually.'

I thought he sounded a bit aggrieved. 'You tell me — you obviously know.'

Derek didn't answer for a long minute, then he replied. 'Here. Right here. Both of them.'

'You mean he is here in the town? Why

didn't he show himself — after he identified the — Grace?' I balked at referring to my aunt as 'the body'.

'He thought it better to remain incognito.'

We were both playing word games now; I was sure I knew the identity of Grace's stepson; for the moment I forgot about the daughter.

Derek sighed. 'It's nearly twenty years since I last saw Grace, but I have happy memories of her. I had some leave due so I thought I would make a trip here and look her up. I only saw her once; we had a drink together — then I was called on to . . . identify her.'

I seized on the least important part of this admission. 'The two whisky glasses — was one yours?'

Derek nodded. 'We spent most of the time discussing you. She was concerned about you and asked me to 'keep an eye on you.' With that in mind I took the empty flat next door to you. Grace pulled a few strings there. Well, more than a few, she was my landlady. She also told me she had left you the rights in her books. She knew my father had left the property to me and his cash to my sister, even so she told me she wanted me to have her business as she thought it might be more of a millstone than a pleasure to you, that you had never been really interested in it.' That was true and I had a stab of guilt that she had known.

'The property?' I repeated stupidly. I seemed intent on latching on to the unimportant or irrelevant.

'Sheep property back in Australia. Grace lived there with us for five years. To tell you the truth it is a bit of a liability now without cash to sink into it. I came here as a sort of last fling while I decided whether to keep on my job and put in a manager, or resign and manage it myself.'

Only five years — why didn't she stay for ever? I wondered; thinking about Grace my mind had skittered over what Derek had been telling me.

'She came back to look after you.'

'Look after me — but . . . ?'

'You are her daughter, Angie. When you were born she let her sister, who had no children and desperately wanted a baby, take you. Grace admitted to me that you were the last thing she wanted at that time. It wasn't meant to be permanent. Grace truly thought it would be the best for everyone, including you. Then they disappeared with you. Grace had a brief note to say they were going to Australia for six months, to see if they liked it. It wasn't till they died that she discovered that that was a lie. They had gone to India as missionaries. They took you and brought you up as their child.'

'I suppose she just accepted that.' It was a statement — not a question. I felt hurt and outraged that I had been handed over like a parcel.

'Not at all. Grace followed you and her sister to Australia — at least she thought she was following you. Unfortunately it is pretty hard to find someone if you are looking on the wrong continent. She spent the next few years searching for you. Did what she could to make a buck, mega bucks in fact. She was at a low ebb when she met Dad, convinced you were lost to her for ever. My mother left him, taking my sister, about a week before Grace arrived as governess to a child no longer there. But she stayed as housekeeper at first; the remoteness of the place probably suited her. I was only a kid and thought they were married. It was only when she left I discovered they weren't. All the same I still think of her as my stepmother. She was good to me and I missed her when she left. I think Dad did too.'

'Why did she leave?' I interrupted to ask.

'She came to rescue you. Someone from the missionary society going through your parents' papers found that you were in England — in a boarding-school.' He paused, remembering. 'She and Dad had an almighty row.' Derek looked sheepish as he told her. 'I was listening outside the door. 'Dad wanted her just to send for you; she insisted she had to go back and rescue you.'

'How did anyone know where Grace was?'

'Apparently her sister knew — somehow or other — and left instructions that in the event of both she and her husband dying Grace was to be notified of your whereabouts.'

I gazed at him stupefied then came out with another irrelevancy. 'You and I are not related then?' The thought gave me a surge of pleasure.

When he didn't reply I wondered if I had perhaps not vocalized my thought. I raised my voice slightly and added, 'But I still don't understand where Tom and Malcolm come into this.'

'Ah, well . . . ' Derek looked at me as if considering whether or not to answer. Then he sighed, frowned slightly and muttered, 'They were blackmailing Grace.'

'That doesn't make sense,' I protested. 'If that was true then surely Grace would have killed one of them?'

'Yes — well — she did try.'

Derek's expression suggested he wondered how I would take this. He looked relieved when I asked, relatively calmly, 'What on earth did they have to blackmail Grace about?'

'Well . . . you.'

'Me?' I could see that there was something here he really didn't want me to know.

I stared at him and said quietly, 'If it concerns me and had to do with Grace's death I have a right to know.'

'They threatened to tell you who you really were.'

I was puzzled. 'But you have just told me. I am quite happy to be Grace's daughter.' I went on staring at him, determined to know the truth.

'Oh, Angie, I suppose you will have to know some time or other. Haven't you ever wondered where Grace got so much money?'

I shrugged. 'Not really, her books — her business?'

Derek shook his head. 'Neither would bring in enough money to pay a blackmailer.' I kept my eyes on his face. 'She was . . . she ran a — a very discreet and expensive establishment.'

I gasped. 'Are you telling me that Grace, my aunt, was a madam?' I laughed. The idea was too absurd. 'Oh no, Derek, I will never believe that! She was the very epitome of an English gentlewoman; she could never have been a — a madam!'

'It was a very exclusive establishment,' Derek repeated, as if that made it OK. 'They were also going to tell you that you were her child, born out of wedlock, not the legitimate daughter of missionaries.'

'I might have weathered the shock.' I remarked drily. Then, wondering somewhat belatedly, I asked, 'Who was my father?'

'He was a well-known businessman in the town. Unfortunately he was already married. He paid Grace well to keep things quiet, then had nothing more to do with her. He's dead now — died not long after you were born,' he added.

'I see.' I was sorry in a way. At the moment I would have liked to confront him, point out the train of events he had triggered off, culminating in Grace's death.

'What about Malcolm?' I asked. 'How does he come into the picture? Why were he and Tom together?'

Derek sighed and looked unhappy, I could see he wanted to drop the subject, but I needed to know everything.

'He wanted to marry you, hoped Grace would encourage you. Sorry, Angie, not for your charms — he prefers boys — but he knew you were Grace's heir. He was Grace's accountant and well aware how wealthy she was. He was also Tom's accountant and knew enough about his affairs to turn him over to the Inland Revenue if he felt so inclined. He knew she had set up Tom in that shop of his, knew about the properties she owned, knew too about her past. All in all he was in a good position to feather his nest very well. To be married to you would be a wonderful smokescreen, or so he thought, for some of his less than salubrious activities. Grace didn't want you in his power.'

'The money — is there still so much around?' I found I was shuddering. I didn't want any of it; it was tainted.

He shook his head and I heard my own sigh of relief.

'There was in the beginning. She invested the money she had made from — well, that she had made — very well. But they got too greedy. Over the years they have consistently bled her. Tom demanded, and got, more and more. He wanted the deeds to the shop but she stood firm, promising only to leave it to him in her will. Your flat and mine are so heavily mortgaged they are more a liability than an asset, as is the place she lived in. Her shop barely paid its way; about all she had was the income from her books.'

He seemed lost in his own thoughts, and I, lost in mine, didn't interrupt them. He sighed after a while, and said, 'She told me that some of the happiest years of her life were when she was living with Dad. Only two things spoiled it: worry about you and fear that he might find out about her past. She told me she daren't push her luck and return when she came back to England to get you. The pity of it was that Dad knew but never let her know he knew. She should have done as Dad begged and just sent for you, as it was as soon as she got back here that Tom was on her back again. Because she refused to pay more, and wouldn't have anything to do with some drug-dealing scheme he and Malcolm had plans to launch, they decided she was expendable. They were waiting for her when she returned home after her dinner with you. Afraid of this, she had taken a small handgun with her; my father had given it to her years ago, but somehow they wrested it off her and one of them brought it down on her head. They wrapped the gun in the scarf she was wearing and took it into the park, threw the gun in the ornamental lake, but it was a bit blustery that night and the scarf got away — they couldn't find it — but you and Billy did.'

'No wonder they had it in for Billy!' I murmured.

'I gather she has used a lot of her real life experiences in her novels, which, no doubt, helps make them so successful. They were convinced she had written some vital information into the last one. That's why they broke into your apartment and went through it.'

We sat in silence for a while. My sadness was softened by his presence; I tried to suppress the thought that he would soon be leaving again for Australia.

I thought I must have expressed my thoughts aloud when he asked, 'Have you ever thought of Australia, Angie?' He went on, without waiting for my reply, 'Grace was very anxious that I should look after you.'

'I don't need 'looking after',' I retorted fiercely, quite forgetting how he had come to my rescue.

'Of course not,' he agreed. 'But you might like to see what she left to come back for you.' His smile was warm, his voice coaxing. Was this, I wondered, some sort of proposal?

'Could Billy come?' I asked, and wondered if that was some sort of acceptance.

'Grace trusted you to look after him; that is why the number of the safe was hidden in his tag.' His arm tightened round me and he murmured against my hair, 'Shall we give it ago?'

My answer was to complete the kiss begun in the police station. The words of my answer were lost but my actions said it all.